Fifth Night
by

Kathi Daley

D1739026

I want to thank the very talented Jessica Fischer for the cover art.

I so appreciate Bruce Curran, who is always ready and willing to answer my cyber questions, and Peggy Hyndman, for helping sleuth out those pesky typos.

And, of course, thanks to the readers and bloggers in my life, who make doing what I do possible.

Thank you to Randy Ladenheim-Gil for the editing.

And finally I want to thank my sister Christy for always lending an ear and my husband Ken for allowing me time to write by taking care of everything else.

Books by Kathi Daley

Come for the murder, stay for the romance.

Zoe Donovan Cozy Mystery:

Halloween Hijinks
The Trouble With Turkeys
Christmas Crazy
Cupid's Curse
Big Bunny Bump-off
Beach Blanket Barbie
Maui Madness
Derby Divas
Haunted Hamlet
Turkeys, Tuxes, and Tabbies
Christmas Cozy
Alaskan Alliance
Matrimony Meltdown
Soul Surrender
Heavenly Honeymoon
Hopscotch Homicide
Ghostly Graveyard
Santa Sleuth
Shamrock Shenanigans
Kitten Kaboodle
Costume Catastrophe
Candy Cane Caper
Holiday Hangover
Easter Escapade
Camp Carter

Trick or Treason
Reindeer Roundup
Hippity Hoppity Homicide – *March 2018*

Zimmerman Academy The New Normal
Ashton Falls Cozy Cookbook

Tj Jensen Paradise Lake Mysteries by Henery Press:

Pumpkins in Paradise
Snowmen in Paradise
Bikinis in Paradise
Christmas in Paradise
Puppies in Paradise
Halloween in Paradise
Treasure in Paradise
Fireworks in Paradise
Beaches in Paradise – *June 2018*

Whales and Tails Cozy Mystery:

Romeow and Juliet
The Mad Catter
Grimm's Furry Tail
Much Ado About Felines
Legend of Tabby Hollow
Cat of Christmas Past
A Tale of Two Tabbies
The Great Catsby
Count Catula
The Cat of Christmas Present
A Winter's Tail
The Taming of the Tabby

Frankencat
The Cat of Christmas Future
Farewell to Felines – *February 2018*

Seacliff High Mystery:
The Secret
The Curse
The Relic
The Conspiracy
The Grudge
The Shadow
The Haunting

Sand and Sea Hawaiian Mystery:
Murder at Dolphin Bay
Murder at Sunrise Beach
Murder at the Witching Hour
Murder at Christmas
Murder at Turtle Cove
Murder at Water's Edge
Murder at Midnight

Writers' Retreat Southern Seashore Mystery:
First Case
Second Look
Third Strike
Fourth Victim
Fifth Night

Rescue Alaska Paranormal Mystery:
Finding Justice

A Tess and Tilly Mystery:
The Christmas Letter
The Valentine Mystery – *February 2018*

Road to Christmas Romance:
Road to Christmas Past

The Writers Retreat Residents

Jillian (Jill) Hanford

Jillian is a dark-haired, dark-eyed, never-married newspaper reporter who moved to Gull Island after her much-older brother, Garrett Hanford, had a stroke and was no longer able to run the resort he'd inherited. Jillian had suffered a personal setback and needed a change in lifestyle, so she decided to run the resort as a writers' retreat while she waited for an opportunity to work her way back into her old life. Since then, she has found a home on Gull Island and has decided to stay and work with Jack running the local newspaper.

Jackson (Jack) Jones

Jack is a dark-haired, blue-eyed, never-married, nationally acclaimed author of hard-core mysteries and thrillers, who is as famous for his good looks and boyish charm as he is for the stories he pens. Despite his success as a novelist, he'd always dreamed of writing for a newspaper, so he gave up his penthouse apartment and bought the failing *Gull Island News*.

George Baxter

George is a writer of traditional whodunit mysteries. He'd been a friend of Garrett Hanford's since they were boys and spent many winters at the resort penning his novels. When he heard the oceanfront resort was going to be used as a writers' retreat, he was one of the first to get on board. George is a distinguished-looking man with gray hair, dark green eyes, and a certain sense of old-fashioned style that many admire.

Clara Kline

Clara is a self-proclaimed psychic who writes fantasy and paranormal mysteries. She wears her long gray hair in a practical braid and favors long, peasant-type skirts and blouses. Clara decided to move to the retreat after she had a vision that she would find her soul mate living within its walls. So far, the only soul mate she has stumbled on to is a cat named Agatha, but it does seem that romance is in the air, so she may yet find the man she has envisioned.

Alex Cole

Alex is a fun and flirty millennial who made his first million writing science fiction when he was just twenty-two. He's the lighthearted jokester of the group who uses his blond-haired, blue-eyed good looks to participate in serial dating. He has the means to live anywhere, but the thought of a writers' retreat seemed quaint and retro, so he decided to expand his base of experience and moved in.

Brit Baxter

Brit is George Baxter's niece. A petite blond pixie and MIT graduate, she decided to make the trip east with her uncle after quitting her job to pursue her dream of writing. Her real strength is in social networking and understanding the dynamics behind the information individuals choose to share on the internet.

Victoria Vance

Victoria is a romance author who lives the life she writes about in her steamy novels. She travels the world and does what she wants to who she wants without ever making an emotional connection. Her raven-black hair accentuates her pale skin and bright green eyes. She's the woman every man fantasizes about but none can conquer. When she isn't traveling the world, she's Jillian's best friend, which is why when Jillian needed her, she gave up her penthouse apartment overlooking Central Park to move into the dilapidated island retreat.

Nicole Carrington

Nicole is a tall and thin true crime author with long dark hair, a pale complexion, and huge brown eyes. She has lived a tragic life and tends to keep to herself, which can make her seem standoffish. Initially, she didn't seem to want to be approached for any reason. It didn't seem she would fit in, but she has shown signs of softening up a bit now that she's gotten to know everyone, and has even agreed to attend a few of the group dinners the writers share from time to time.

Garrett Hanford

Garrett isn't a writer, but he owns the resort and is becoming one of the gang. He had a stroke that ended his ability to run the resort as a family vacation spot. He has lived on Gull Island his entire life and has a lot to offer the Mystery Mastermind Group.

Townsfolk

Deputy Rick Savage

Rick is not only the island's main source of law enforcement, he's a volunteer force unto himself. He cares about the island and its inhabitants and is willing to do what needs to be done to protect that which he loves. He's a single man in his thirties who seldom has time to date despite his devilish good looks, which most believe could land him any woman he wants.

Mayor Betty Sue Bell

Betty Sue is a homegrown Southern lady who owns a beauty parlor called Betty Boop's Beauty Salon. She can be flirty and sassy, but when her town or its citizens are in trouble, she turns into a barracuda. She has a Southern flare that will leave you laughing, but when there's a battle to fight, she's the one you most want in your corner.

Gertie Newsome

Gertie is the owner of Gertie's on the Wharf. Southern born and bred, she believes in the magic of the South and the passion of its people. She shares her home with a ghost named Mortie who has been a regular part of her life for over thirty years. She's friendly, gregarious, and outspoken, unafraid to take on anyone or anything she needs to protect those she loves.

Meg Collins

Meg is a volunteer at the island museum and the organizer of the turtle rescue squad. Some feel the island and its wildlife are her life, but Meg has a soft spot for island residents like Jill and the writers who live with her.

Barbara Jean Freeman

Barbara is an outspoken woman with a tendency toward big hair and loud colors. She's a friendly sort with a propensity toward gossip who owns a bike shop in town.

Brooke Johnson

Brooke is a teacher and mother who works hard in her spare time as volunteer coordinator for the community. She met Jack and Jill when she was a suspect in the first case they tackled.

Sully

Sully is a popular islander who owns the local bar and offers lots of information about the goings-on in the community. When Blackbeard manages to escape for a day on the town, one of the first stops he always makes is to see his buddy Sully.

Quinten Davenport

Quinten is a retired Los Angeles County Medical Examiner who is currently dating Gertie. Although retired, Quinten is more than happy to help the Mystery Mastermind Group when they need a medical opinion, and his presence provides stability to   them.

The Victim

Bobby Boston

Bobby was a twenty-nine-year-old firefighter with the Gull Island Fire Department. Six months ago, he was found dead in his car by his twenty-five-year-old wife, Abby. It appears as if Bobby committed suicide. He left a note stating he had been responsible for a man's death and was unable to continue living with his guilt.

The Suspects and Witnesses

Abby Boston

Abby married Bobby four years ago, just before moving to Gull Island, where he had gotten a job with the Gull Island firehouse. Initially, Abby worked as a preschool teacher, but two years ago, her sister, Tammy, and Tammy's husband, Toby, were killed in an auto accident. Abby was named legal guardian for Abby's four children, aged three to ten, quit her job, and became a full-time mom. Seven months ago, just a month before Bobby died, Abby found out she was pregnant with the couple's first biological child. Now, Abby is due to deliver in just seven weeks. The company that held Bobby's life insurance policy has refused to pay because he committed suicide, and Abby's small savings are about to run out. She has received a letter of eviction from the bank and is desperate to prove Bobby didn't commit suicide before she, her nieces and nephews, and her unborn child, are thrown out on the street.

Laurie Olson

Laurie, Abby's best friend, insists Abby and Bobby were a committed couple who had simply been suffering a rough patch when she became pregnant unexpectedly. She does not believe Bobby committed suicide

Sam Petrie

Sam is a fellow firefighter. He was hired shortly before Bobby, and while the two got along, they both were ambitious and had entered into a rivalry of sorts. Sam claims Bobby was already stressed with the responsibility of raising his wife's nieces and nephews, and when he found out about the baby, it put him over the edge.

Captain Roy Oliver

Captain Oliver was Bobby's fire chief. At the time of the investigation of Bobby's death, he told the deputy assigned to investigate the case that Bobby was a hard worker and a good man, but he had been dealing with some severe emotional distress for several weeks before the beginning of an arson spree.

Pop Seaton

Pop was the first victim of the arsonist. He owned a fishing boat that was destroyed while it was in dry dock for repair. No one was injured, and Pop had insurance to replace the boat he had lost.

Jasper Wells

Jasper was the second victim of the Gull Island arsonist. He lost a barn that was, fortunately, empty because it had been undergoing renovation. No one was injured, and Jasper had insurance to rebuild the barn.

Hillary Tisdale

Hillary owned the local bakeshop until it burned to the ground on the third night of the arson spree. The bakeshop was closed, so there were no casualties, but the building was completely destroyed. Luckily, Hillary had adequate insurance, which she has used to relocate.

Hannah Smith

Hannah was the fourth victim of the Gull Island arsonist. She was a struggling artist who had set up a studio in the detached garage behind her house. The artwork and the building were destroyed, but the house was saved, and no one was injured. Hannah had recently been invited to show her work at a gallery in New York, so she'd taken out an insurance policy on the paintings just days before the fire.

David Long

David was the only human casualty of the Gull Island arsonist. On the fifth night of the spree, the arsonist burned to the ground the house belonging to a family who were vacationing in Los Angeles. David was a friend of the family who was staying in the house and was unable to get out before smoke overtook him. It was generally assumed, given the fact that the arsonist seemed to have chosen unoccupied buildings with adequate insurance, that he didn't know the house was occupied and didn't mean to kill the man sleeping inside. The suicide note left by Bobby seemed to confirm this.

Chapter 1

Monday, January 22

"Hi, everyone," the young woman with a rounded belly on a stick-thin frame, long blond hair, and large haunted eyes, began. "My name is Abby Boston. Brit asked me to come here tonight to tell my story." She nervously glanced at Brit Baxter, the youngest member of the Mystery Mastermind Group, which met every Monday evening at the Gull Island Writers' Retreat. It looked like the poor girl might flee, but Brit smiled encouragingly. Abby nodded at her, and then turned once more to face the group. "As you may know, my husband, Bobby, died six months ago, leaving me to care for my nieces and nephews on my own." Abby rubbed her huge stomach. "Baby Tammy, to be named for my late sister, will be joining us shortly, and I'm terrified. You see," Abby glanced around the room, her eyes filling with tears, "after Bobby died, I got behind on my mortgage. I received a notice from the bank last week saying I either needed to get my loan up to date or vacate the house." Abby's eyes met mine. My heart was breaking for the young woman who had lost first her sister and then her husband. "I don't have the money to pay the bank and I don't know where the kids and I will go if we lose the house. I spoke to Brit about my dilemma and she said you all might be able to help."

"Are you looking for a donation?" asked Alex Cole, a fun and flirty millennial who made his first million writing science fiction when he was just twenty-two.

"No, sir." Abby shook her head vigorously. "I'm not looking for a handout. The kids and I will find a way to make it on our own."

"So why are you here?" asked Victoria Vance, a romance novelist and my best friend.

"Bobby had an insurance policy. He took it out when my sister was killed and her kids came to live with us. He worked as a firefighter, and a fisherman on his days off. Both are high-risk jobs, and he wanted to be sure we'd be taken care of if anything happened to him. The problem is that the insurance company is refusing to pay. There's a stipulation in the policy that they won't in cases of suicide."

That seemed a pretty standard condition to me. "What exactly are you asking?" I wondered.

"I need for you, Ms. Hanford, and your group, to prove Bobby didn't commit suicide. I need you to prove he was murdered."

I paused to consider her request. I didn't know a lot about the case, but I did remember when Bobby Boston died. It seemed Deputy Rick Savage, Vikki's boyfriend and a friend of the group, had been the one who investigated, and he'd determined there was no evidence to rule the case anything other than a suicide. Of course, I hadn't known Rick back then; I'd just moved to the island when Abby's husband had been found dead, so I didn't have the background to have a firm opinion about it.

"I know Jill and the rest of you probably think it will be a long shot to prove a man who died by asphyxiation after leaving a suicide note was really murdered," Brit added. "But it's the only shot Abby has. She shared with me the details relating to the series of events leading up to her husband's death and I really think she may be on to something. It does appear as if he might have been set up to take the fall for the real arsonist."

"Okay." I looked around at the people gathered. I could sense their sympathy for the young woman who seemed to be shouldering the weight of the world; and their trepidation at becoming involved in a case that, certainly on the surface, appeared to be cut and dried. "I'd love to help Abby, but I think we should hear the rest of the story before we decide." I looked at Abby. "Please continue."

Her face became even paler than before. I could imagine how she must feel, standing in front of our group pleading her case while we decided whether we believed her story. I hadn't meant to make her feel like she was on trial, but I was pretty sure that was exactly how she did. "On second thought," I glanced at Brit, "maybe you should tell us what you know, and Abby can fill in where necessary."

Brit smiled at me with a look of thanks. "That would probably work the best." She turned to Abby.

"Why don't you sit down next to me so you'll be close by if I need to verify anything?" Abby looked like she'd been granted a reprieve and did exactly as Brit had suggested. Once Abby was seated, Brit looked around the room, making eye contact with each of the seven people present before she continued. "Abby's husband, Bobby, worked as a firefighter for the Gull Island Fire Department. Beginning in May of this past year, there were a series of fires, which eventually were ruled to be arson. In all, there were five fires that burned down five structures over a six-week period."

"I remember that," said Jack Jones, my boyfriend and the owner of the *Gull Island News*. "Initially, he was referred to as the gentleman arsonist because all the fires were set at insured and unoccupied structures. While the fires caused inconvenience, the sites seemed to have been selected to cause minimal harm."

"That's true," Brit confirmed. "Until the last one. On the fifth night, a home was burned to the ground. The family who lived there were away on vacation, and it was assumed that, like the other four fires, the fifth would result in no casualties. The problem was, a friend of the family was staying in the house, seemingly unbeknownst to anyone on the island. He died of smoke inhalation." The group remained silent while we waited for Brit to continue. "A week after the fifth fire, Abby found Bobby dead in their garage when she got back from shopping. He was sitting in the driver's seat of his car, with a note claiming responsibility for the death of the man who'd died in the last fire beside him. The note said he was unable to live with the guilt of having been responsible for the man's death."

"And you don't think that was what happened?" asked George Baxter, Brit's uncle, a mystery writer and the most senior member of our group.

"Abby's certain her husband would never set the fires or willingly leave her to raise five children on her own. She believes the person who was really responsible for the fires killed Bobby and made it look like he was the one behind them. I can't claim to have any empirical proof one way or the other, but after speaking with Abby, I have reason to believe she may be on to something. That's why we're asking the Mystery Mastermind Group to look in to the situation."

The group had been formed to look in to old cases that had been closed but seemed to still have unanswered questions. Abby's case seemed like a worthwhile one to take on, but I wanted to leave that up to everyone. It was going to be hard to discuss the case with Abby sitting among us, so I called for a break, at which time I suggested to Brit that it might be best if Abby left. We would make a decision and Brit could let her know the following morning.

I put on a fresh pot of coffee while Brit walked Abby out to her car. The case with which they'd presented us had the potential to become a highly emotional one for everyone involved. I hoped everyone, if they agreed to take it on, would be up to the task of finding the truth, even if it turned out it wasn't what we were looking for.

"What do you think?" I asked after coffee cups had been refreshed and the group had reconvened.

"My sense is that Abby's telling the truth," Clara Kline, a self-proclaimed psychic, spoke up. "I don't have a sense about her husband and his role in the arson cases, but if you're asking if I'm voting to take on her case, I say we should."

I glanced at my half brother, Garrett Hanford, who was sitting next to Clara. He wasn't a writer, but he owned the resort where the retreat was located and was therefore an honorary member of the group. "Garrett?"

"I'm not sure if I should get a vote, but I'm in if I do. I don't have any idea whether Abby's husband killed himself, but I can't help but ache for her and the huge burden she has to bear. If there's a way to help, I'm up for doing whatever needs to be done."

"I'm in as well," said George.

"Me too." Vikki glanced around the room with a look of determination on her face. I could sense Abby's story had torn at her tender heart.

I saw Alex turn to look at Brit. He was a great guy, but he tended to be a bit more analytical than the rest of us, and slower to commit. "Abby's in a tough spot and I think we all want to help her, but is there any evidence at all to support a conclusion different from the obvious one?"

"I have no idea whether Bobby killed himself or if, as Abby suspects, he was murdered and then framed for the arsons. But I do know Abby's a very nice woman who has been through a lot and is in a tough spot. If our looking in to her husband's death gives her even a small chance of saving her house, I think we should do it."

Alex leaned back in his chair and crossed his arms over his chest, taking a moment to contemplate the situation. "Was the suicide note handwritten?" he eventually asked.

"Typewritten," Brit replied. "There was a signature that did appear to be Bobby's, but we all know there are ways to forge signatures without much effort these days."

Alex narrowed his gaze. I could sense his hesitation and I was certain Brit could as well.

"Please? For Abby," Brit added.

Alex shrugged. "Okay. I don't have a lot going on right now. I'm in."

"I'm in as well," Jack said. He sat forward in his chair, resting his forearms on his thighs. "It seems the first order of business should be to deal with the bank. We need to buy ourselves enough time to look in to things. I'll talk to the bank manager tomorrow."

I smiled at Jack, who was sitting across the room with his new puppy, Kizmet, at his feet. He was such a wonderful, caring man who really put himself out if he came across a person in need.

"Okay," I said, "I guess we have our first case of the new year. Jack and I will do some preliminary work tomorrow, and then we'll get together again to assign tasks. Can everyone meet back here tomorrow evening?"

"Oh, I can't do tomorrow." Brit flinched. "I have my writing class. I can do Wednesday."

"Does Wednesday work for everyone else?" I asked.

"Are you cooking?" Alex asked.

"I'd be happy to."

"Then I'll be here. Right now, however, I have a date."

"A date?" Brit asked. "Is there a new special someone in your life?"

Alex just winked, then left the room.

After everyone had returned to their cabin or room in the main house, Jack and I took Kizzy for a walk on the beach. She was an adorable golden retriever puppy Jack and I had found on the beach just before Christmas. While we didn't know her exact age, we estimated she must be around five months old. I'd never been much of a pet person, and adopting a dog hadn't been anywhere on my radar, but in the month Jack and I had shared parenting responsibilities for the easygoing yet rambunctious pup, she had firmly wormed her way into my heart.

"Kizzy did really well at the meeting tonight," I said as we walked hand in hand. "She didn't try to chase Agatha once." Agatha was Clara's cat, who didn't have a lot of patience for people, except Clara, or other pets.

"I've been working with her. She's a smart little girl. I think she's going to turn out to be something very special."

I watched Kizzy run up and down the beach ahead of us. It was such a peaceful evening. It had turned chilly, but the sky was clear, and there were a million stars overhead. The Turtle Cove Resort, where I had established the Gull Island Writers' Retreat, had been in Garrett's family for generations. While the resort initially had been run as a family vacation spot, I'd changed things up a bit after Garrett had his stroke and he asked me to run things. The writers' colony was situated on a peninsula that featured ocean and sandy beaches to the east and marshland to the west. It truly was an exceptional piece of property, and I considered myself lucky to live here. I currently lived in the main house with Garrett and Clara, while George, Alex, Brit, and Vikki each had their own cabin. Jack, who had more money than he knew what to do with, lived in a huge mansion overlooking the sea, but he had plans to build his own cabin on the grounds so he could be closer to the rest of us.

In addition to the members of the Mystery Mastermind Group, there were three other writers living in cabins. Nicole Carrington is a reclusive true crime writer who initially insisted on being left completely alone but has recently begun to soften up a bit and has even occasionally joined us when we get together for dinner. We also have two temporary residents, a historian who's staying with us while he completes a book on the area, and a romance writer, who rented one of the newly refurbished cabins for the winter to write the first in a series of steamy novels.

"Do you really think you can convince the bank manager to hold off on the foreclosure while we investigate?"

"I do," Jack answered. "It may take some negotiation, but in the long run, the bank has nothing to gain by proceeding with the foreclosure process and everything to gain by working out a way for Abby to resume the payments and remain in her home."

I lay my head on Jack's shoulder. "It's nice of you to go the extra mile. I know you're already superbusy this week with the remodel of the newspaper office."

Jack slipped an arm around my shoulders and pulled me close. "It's not a problem at all, but I might need you to be available to babysit if both the paneling guy and the cabinet guy want to show up at the same time again."

"Are they still arguing over who should have access to the lobby and conference room first?"

"Like eight-year-olds. I'd hire someone else, but there aren't a lot of choices on the island."

"Doesn't it make sense that the paneling should go in first and then the cabinets should go over the paneling?"

"Makes sense to me, but the cabinet guy insists he needs to install the cabinets on bare wall minus the paneling, and the paneling guy says if the cabinets go up first, he'll have to cut around everything. I think I'm going to shop around a bit before I make a decision about who to hire when I build the cabin."

"How are the plans for that going?" I asked. I hadn't been sure it was a good idea for Jack to sell his mansion and move into a small cabin on the beach, but the more we talked about it, the more excited I'd become. Not only would Jack be living only footsteps away from me, but I would have more access to Kizzy as well. Of course, the downside of that living arrangement was that I'd recently started working with Jack at the newspaper. Would there be a point at which so much togetherness evolved into too much togetherness?

"They're going well," Jack answered. "If all goes according to plan, I should be able to break ground next month. I want the shell up before the turtles arrive. I figure I'll take a break from the construction during nesting season, so they won't be disturbed."

"I'm sure the turtles will appreciate that, as will the members of the turtle rescue squad."

Jack picked up a stick and threw it for Kizzy. "I'm not in a hurry, and I'm committed to doing this project in as environmentally conscious a way as possible. That reminds me: did you ever get the interview you were hoping for with the developer who wants to build condos over the wetlands?"

"It's all set for tomorrow afternoon. I've looked at his project and it's insane. I can't understand why anyone would want to build housing over water."

"He wants to rent the units to tourists. His vision is to build everything up on supports and raised walkways, sort of like the huts over the ocean in places like Bali. I get why he thinks the idea will be popular with tourists, but the environmentalists are never going to go for it. It seems to me he's wasting his time, but I guess it's his to waste."

I frowned. "Yeah, I guess. In my experience, however, most developers are accomplished businessmen who don't go after projects they know will never fly. Maybe he knows something we don't."

"Perhaps. We'll need to keep an eye on things as they develop."

Kizzy ran up to us and dropped her stick at our feet. I bent down and picked it up, then threw it as hard as I could down the beach, and Kizzy took off running again. "If he does pursue the project, it's going to become a hot-button issue, which will probably sell a lot of newspapers."

"Very true." Jack turned his head slightly and gave me a quick kiss on the cheek. "I have some news of my own."

"Oh? And what's that?"

"My agent called to tell me that one of the publishing houses I work with is interested in doing more books in the series I wrote for them. In my own mind, I'd already wrapped it up, so I said I wasn't interested in doing any more books in that series. Now the publisher is offering an obscene advance, and she's pushing me to make a commitment."

"I would think a decision like that should be up to you. I mean, your agent works for you, not the other way around."

Jack nodded. "In theory, sure. But at times these negotiations can become complicated because…"

"Your agent is your mother," I remembered.

"Exactly. She's very committed to getting me to change my mind and has decided to come for a visit."

"I see. And when will she be here?"

"The day after tomorrow."

I paused before answering. I had a feeling the way I reacted to this news could be important and I didn't want to get it wrong. "You have a lot going on, and a visit from either a mother or an agent is probably going to add a lot of stress to your schedule, though I'd be excited to meet your mother. I'm sure if she raised an amazing guy like you, she must be pretty amazing herself."

Jack lifted a shoulder. "She's amazing, but she's also driven and can be relentless when it comes to getting what she wants. I love my mother, and I don't think I made a mistake asking her to be my agent when I was a young man publishing my first book. I probably owe her my career. But now that I own the newspaper and am building a life here on the island, I realize I need to cut back on my fiction output. The problem is that Mom sees the newspaper as a temporary distraction. She talks like I'm having some sort of midlife crisis and the newspaper is a shiny red

Corvette. I'd love to have some time to catch up with Mom, but I have a feeling the entire visit is going to be me battling my agent."

"You're in a tough spot."

Jack let out a long breath. "I really am. I never should have allowed her to integrate herself so firmly into my professional life. I'm afraid if I refuse to do what my agent wants, I'll lose the fairly amiable relationship I've always had with my mother."

"If there's anything at all I can do to help, just ask."

Jack looked toward Kizzy, who was chasing the waves. "I might need you to keep Kizzy while my mom's here. She'll be staying at my house and isn't a fan of four-legged creatures of any kind."

"I'd love to keep Kizzy for a few days. I'm sure she'll miss you, but it'll give us a chance to bond. And if you need a place to run away to, my door is always open."

"I'm glad to hear that. In the meantime, how would you like to stay at my house tonight? I'm afraid we won't have much time together once Mom gets here."

"I'd love to. Just let me grab a few things."

Jack and I returned to the house, where he wiped the sand from Kizzy's paws while I ran upstairs to grab an overnight bag with basic toiletries and clean clothes for the following morning. Although I hadn't let on, I was somewhat nervous about Jack's mother's upcoming visit. She was important to Jack and Jack was important to me, so I wanted us to get along. When Jack spoke of his mother, it was with a tone that revealed both admiration and trepidation. I wasn't sure what to make of that. He'd been just nineteen when he'd written his first best seller. His mother, who had a background in marketing, had quit her job to be his agent. Jack's writing had always been a huge success, and I was sure at least a part of that was due to his mother's work, but I worried what an overinvolved mother could do to our still-new relationship.

Jack seemed to be his own man, capable of making his own decisions, but I had enough of my own mother issues to understand that when it came to family matters that should be easy, they could have a way of becoming complicated in no time.

Chapter 2

Tuesday, January 23

The next morning, Jack headed to the bank to discuss Abby's mortgage, while I went to the newspaper office to babysit the contractors. I couldn't see why the two men, both professionals, couldn't come to some sort of an agreement on their own, but based on the bickering I overheard from the adjacent room, an amiable negotiation didn't seem to be on the table. After twenty minutes of listening to their quarreling I'd had enough. I stormed into the conference room in full irate-female mode and told them they had ten minutes to work it out, and if they couldn't, they could pack up their stuff and get out.

It took only five minutes for me to hear the sweet sound of hammering. Jack was handy with a hammer; I didn't understand why he wasn't simply handling the remodel on his own. Of course, it had been a busy couple of months, and he'd been trying to juggle all the various parts of his life for quite some time. Most of the time, he made it look easy, but when I stopped to think about it, it was remarkable the way he managed to produce two *New York Times* best sellers a year while running the newspaper and spending quite a bit of time investigating the seemingly endless series of mysteries our group had found reason to dig in to. And I supposed at some point he was going to have to go on a book tour. His newest mystery was releasing next month, and while he hadn't said as much, I fully expected he would need to be away from Gull Island for at least some time.

I guess it was a good thing Jack had brought me on as a partner of sorts. I loved the life I was building on Gull Island, but he knew I missed being part of a newspaper. Sure, his weekly could never compare to the paper I'd last worked for, but writing articles about bake sales and community events seemed to fill the hole that had been left in my life when I moved from New York to South Carolina.

"Is that hammering I hear?" Jack said as he placed a white take-out bag from the local bakery in front of me.

"It is," I confirmed. "You should have both cabinets and paneling done by the end of the day."

Jack smiled. "That's great. How'd you get them to work it out? I've been trying for days."

"There's nothing a man hates more than a woman on the verge of hysteria."

He laughed. "It's hard to imagine you convincing anyone you were bordering on hysteria, but I appreciate whatever you did to get things back on track."

"How'd your meeting go at the bank?" I wondered.

"Well, Abby is five months behind on her mortgage payments. I paid half of what she owed, and the bank agreed to restructure the remainder into the balance of the mortgage. I even worked it out so her next payment isn't due for a month. Hopefully, we can prove Bobby didn't commit suicide and she can get the money she's owed from the insurance company by then. If not, I'll help her out if need be."

"You really are a special guy."

Jack shrugged. "I have the money, and she seems like a good kid. I thought she seemed like she might not welcome a handout, so I asked the bank not to mention the payment, just let her know they'd reworked the mortgage to give her the time she needed to work out her finances."

"Now all we need to do is find the real arsonist and expose them as a killer."

He opened the take-out bag and pulled out a muffin. He set it on a napkin, then poured us both a cup of coffee from the pot. "I'm not saying it will be easy, but it doesn't seem any harder than any of the other cases we've taken on. I've been thinking about a plan of attack, and I think we should start by hearing what Rick has to say."

Deputy Rick Savage was the deputy assigned to the island and had become a friend of those in the Mastermind group when he began dating Vikki. He didn't come to the meetings, but he was usually able to help, at least to an extent.

"That's a good idea," I replied. "Question is, what should we do about Mutt and Jeff?" I tilted my head toward the room where the two men were working. "I think they plan to be here for most of the day."

"I'll talk to them. As long as they agree to play nice, I think we can leave them alone for a while."

Jack spoke to the contractors and secured their promises that they'd work together to complete the work by the end of the day. Then we headed to the sheriff's office. We weren't sure Rick would be there, but we'd found it was usually best to just drop in. If he wasn't around, we could always move on to plan b.

"It looks like the two of you are on a mission," Rick said when we appeared in his small office after passing through the reception area.

"New case," I said.

"Another closed one you feel shouldn't have been?" Rick asked.

"Yes and no," I replied. "We're helping Abby Boston look in to the death of her husband Bobby." I walked further into the office and sat down on one of the two chairs on the opposite side of the desk from Rick. "I'm aware you were the one who looked in to the matter, and I've been told you didn't find anything that indicated Bobby hadn't set the fires and then killed himself. But Abby is certain he would never do what the note he left seems to indicate. It's important to her and her family to find the truth."

"What if the truth is exactly what the investigation turned up?" Rick asked.

"Then Abby will know she's done what she can. Even if it does turn out that Bobby killed himself, she won't be any worse off than she is now. However, if we can find something—anything—that might convince you to reopen the case, it could mean Abby will receive the insurance money she so desperately needs."

Rick didn't answer.

"She's a twenty-five-year-old woman who's been left to raise four children plus one on the way on her own. She's all alone in the world and needs our help."

Rick ran a hand through his hair. "Okay. I'll help if I can. The sheriff put a lot of pressure on me to close the case at the time, though it did feel a little off. What do you know at this point?"

"Not a lot," I admitted. "Abby attended the Mastermind meeting last night, and between her and Brit, we have a general idea of what occurred. They mentioned the five fires and that a man died in the fifth one. They also described the circumstances under which Abby found her husband's body. We haven't had a chance to come up with a plan of action, but we figured we'd start by speaking to you."

Rick put his hands on his desk and pushed himself to his feet. He glanced at the clock, then grabbed his coat from the rack. "I haven't eaten yet and I'm starving. How about you buy me lunch and I'll tell you what I know?"

"Deal."

The three of us headed over to Gertie's on the Wharf. The owner, Gertie, was a longtime local who always knew the island gossip and served meals that reminded you of home. I first met her shortly after arriving on the island, and in the months since, she'd become one of my closest friends. Gertie had a natural if not blunt way about her. Not one to spare words, she was the sort who'd look you in the eye and tell you exactly what she thought. I liked that.

Jack had driven, so when we arrived at the wharf he parked in front of the restaurant and the three of us climbed out. Jack led the way, while we followed at a slightly slower pace. The marina that was serviced by the wharf where Gertie's was located was busy in the summer, but during the winter months there were only a few fishing boats tied to the series of buoys that extended out to the sea. A pelican that had been sitting on a post near the door to the restaurant flew away as we approached.

"Who died?" Gertie asked as we walked in.

"Why do you think someone died?" I asked as I slipped off my jacket and hung it on one of the hooks provided for just that purpose.

Gertie made a clucking sound, shaking her head all the while. "I may not know everything there is to know, but when the three of you get together in the middle of a workday, something's goin' on."

Jack led us to a booth in the back, by the window overlooking the marina. It was late for breakfast and early for lunch, so the cafe was empty of customers. During the summer and on the weekends, the place was packed from opening to closing, but on a weekday during the winter, only a few locals stopped by at this time.

"No one died," Rick answered. "At least not recently. I'm helping Jack and Jill with one of their projects."

"Uh-huh. And what project might that be?" Gertie asked as she handed us menus.

"We're looking in to Bobby Boston's death on behalf of his widow," I said as I settled into the booth next to Jack.

"Been wonderin' when someone was going to take some initiative and help that poor woman." Gertie glanced at Rick. "I done tried to provide some relevant insight at the time, but it seems our good deputy here wasn't interested in what ol' Gertie had to say."

"You told me that Mortie said Bobby was murdered."

"It's a true fact," she insisted.

"Maybe. But I don't think a ghost no one but you can see is going to be the sort of witness who can sway the sheriff to change his mind."

Gertie poured us each a cup of coffee without bothering to ask if we wanted any. It was a cold day and the coffee smelled wonderful, so I took a sip as I waited for Gertie to continue. "Mortie's testimony might not convince the sheriff that he's barkin' up the wrong tree, but that doesn't mean you shouldn't listen to what he has to say."

"What did he have to say?" I asked.

"Mortie done told me the fires were started with a very specific purpose in mind. He said the cops were so busy lookin' for evidence of some sort, they totally missed seeing the underlyin' motive."

"The motive?" I asked.

"Who stood to gain something. Can't rightly see that Bobby stood to gain anything by burnin' down five structures."

"Mortie has a point." I looked at Rick.

He looked down at the menu, then set it aside to focus his attention on me. "We considered the motive during the investigation. Initially, I thought one of the victims of the fires might be the arsonist. Every structure that was burned was very well insured. As far as I could tell, except for the man who perished in the last fire—and Bobby and his family, of course—it appeared everyone involved was better off afterward than before the fires occurred."

I frowned as I tried to digest this detail. "The idea that one of the victims was the arsonist makes sense, actually. Why did you drop that line of reasoning?"

"I couldn't find a single piece of evidence to support the theory. There were five totally independent victims who seemingly had nothing in common other than that they were well insured. They had policies with different insurance companies, and none of the five seemed to know any of the others. Additionally, in every case, the owner of the structure was off the island when the fire took place."

"Didn't the fact that they were all off the island seem odd to you?" Jack asked.

"It did at first, but then I realized the arsonist intentionally targeted structures that were unoccupied. It tracks that they looked for targets where the owner was away for some reason. I imagine that decreased the chance they'd stop by and become an unwitting victim." Rick looked at Gertie. "I knew you were disappointed I didn't do more to act on Mortie's tip, but at the time I did what I felt I could."

"Uh-huh."

Rick opened his menu again and gave it another quick glance. "I'd like the chicken fried steak with mashed potatoes."

Gertie was giving him somewhat of a dirty look, but she pulled out her pad and wrote down his order. I wasn't all that hungry, so I ordered a bowl of soup and Jack chose a sandwich.

"I think not paying as much attention to Mortie's tip as Gertie felt you should has landed you in the doghouse," I said to Rick as she went into the kitchen.

"I seem to spend a lot of time in the doghouse when it comes to Gertie. I know she means well, but everything is so random with her. Either something is a fact or it isn't. A tip provided by someone who's been dead for over thirty years isn't a fact. The sheriff would have laughed me clean off the island if I'd gone to him with it."

I unfolded my napkin and set it in my lap. "I'll agree you were in a tough spot, but now that we're looking in to things again for Abby, I don't see how it would hurt to keep Mortie's tip in mind."

Rick lifted a brow.

"I'm not saying Mortie is definitely real or that he's definitely living in Gertie's house, but I'm not saying he isn't either. His tips have helped us out in the past," I pointed out.

Rick smiled a crooked little half smile. I could see he didn't believe in Mortie, which was fine; he didn't need to believe in him to make use of the tips he provided.

"Returning to the facts as we know them," Jack joined in, "assuming you were correct and none of the victims were responsible for the fires, I think we need to ask ourselves, other than the victims, who else had motive?"

"No idea." Rick shook a packet of sugar, tore off the top, and dumped it in his coffee. "Part of the reason the sheriff insisted on closing the case was because we had a confession and absolutely zero other suspects. If there had been other leads, we would have followed them, but there just weren't any."

"How about the fires themselves?" Jack asked. "Was there a signature?"

"You're thinking the fires might not have been set by the same person?" Rick stirred his coffee, then took a sip.

"It's a possibility," Jack said.

"Yeah," I agreed. "Maybe we're looking at a *Strangers on a Train* sort of thing. All five victims might have been off the island when their own structure went up in flames, but I'd be willing to bet they weren't all off the island when *all* the fires occurred."

Rick drummed his fingers on the table. "That's an interesting idea. It does seem a bit too coincidental that not only were all the structures that burned insured but they were *very well* insured by different companies. If one company had written all the policies, the inspector would have taken a very close look at them. But because each company was only on the hook for one fire, only a cursory investigation was conducted."

"Okay, so suppose the five seemingly unconnected victims were connected in some way," I jumped in, warming up to the idea. "Maybe victim one, the boat owner, is in a bar whining that his boat is in dry dock and he can't afford to fix it. Victim number two, the man who lost the barn that was in the process of a remodel, jumped in, saying he had a remodel that had gotten away from him and he couldn't afford to finish it. Both men are crying in their drinks and they get to talking. At some point, they realize they would both be better off if the money-sucking shackle around their neck burned to the ground and they were able to collect the insurance money. They realize if they burn their own structure, they'll become the primary suspect, so they agree to burn down each other's property."

"That makes sense, but there were five structures involved, not two," Rick said.

"So maybe the guy with the boat was buddies with the bakeshop owner and she decided to get in on the plan. Maybe she knew the artist and invited her to join them, and maybe one of them knew the owner of the house that burned down. All we really need to do is find out how any one of the victims is linked to any other one. They don't necessarily have had to all know each other before the plan was put into action."

Gertie returned with our meals. She set the food down but lingered next to the table.

"Seems like a long shot," Rick said as he stirred gravy into his mashed potatoes.

"Maybe, but it gives us a starting point," I argued.

I could see by the look on his face that Rick was thinking about it. It would be a lot of work to find all the links and prove them, but I felt a whole lot more hopeful now than I had when we first arrived.

"Do you have copies of the reports from the fire marshal?" Jack asked.

"I do."

"Why don't the three of us meet again tonight to go over them, as well as everything else in the sheriff's department's file," Jack suggested.

"The three of us?" Gertie complained. "This whole thing came about because of Mortie's input. I want in."

I glanced at Rick. He shrugged.

"Okay, the four of us," I agreed.

"What about Quinten?" Gertie asked. "He might be able to help."

Quinten Davenport was a retired medical examiner and Gertie's gentleman friend.

"Okay, the five of us," I amended.

"You may as well make it six," Rick said. "I have a date with Vikki tonight. She isn't going to be happy if I cancel on her without asking her to join us."

"Fine by me," I said.

"Let's meet at my house," Jack offered. "I'll have dinner brought in."

By the time we finished our lunch, I felt we had a plan to tackle the mystery head-on.

Rick went back to his office, Jack went back to the paper, and I headed to the center of town for my interview with Derek King, the man who wanted to build huts over the marshland. King was staying at the Gull Island Inn, so we'd arranged to meet in the inn's business center, which had a long table along one wall with computers and printers and a round table in the middle for meetings.

"Mr. King." I held out my hand to the tall, thin man with a thick head of brown hair that hung long in the front, partially covering his wire-rimmed glasses. "My name is Jillian Hanford. We spoke on the phone."

"Yes, I've been expecting you. Please have a seat."

I sat down at the round table and King sat next to me.

"I understand you're interested in my project."

I paused as I considered how to delicately let him know I was interested in his project only because I thought it was nuts and would make an interesting article. "I've heard you're proposing to build huts on a raised platform over the marshland on the west side of the island."

"That's correct."

I took out a small notepad and pen, prepared to take notes. "Isn't most of that land publicly owned?"

"Much of it is, but the piece of marsh I'm looking to build on is part of the Littleton estate."

I tapped my lower lip with the pen. "The Littleton estate? I'm new to the area and I'm afraid I'm not familiar with that particular property."

"Marcus Littleton bought up large plots of land back in the thirties. At the time, his holdings constituted over sixty percent of the total land mass of the island, which was mostly uninhabited back then because the only way to reach it was via private boat. During the fifties, the ferry began to stop on the island and the first resort was built, raising the value of the land and opening the door to additional development. Littleton loved the island but was a businessman first, so he began selling off chunks of his acreage for a premium price. Currently, the Littleton family owns just two hundred acres, including forty of marshland. I've offered the family a very good price for sixty acres of land including the forty acres of marsh, contingent on my ability to obtain a permit to build over the marsh."

"So the entire resort you hope to build would be on a platform above the marsh?" I asked.

"The parking area as well as the restaurant and clubhouse would be built on the twenty acres that isn't marsh. My proposal calls for a series of hutlike structures joined one to each other with raised walkways."

I sat back and looked at him. "What about plumbing and electric?"

"I've included the pipes and conduit network that would be required to service the individual units in my plans. I can assure you, I've thought this through quite thoroughly."

I leaned forward on the table so my forearms rested in front of me, then absentmindedly clicked my pen open and closed as I tried to wrap my head around this. I supposed he'd come up with a way to develop the wetlands; the problem, in my opinion, was that the wetlands shouldn't be developed at all. "Have you done any work on the permit process?" I asked.

"I've had a few meetings with men and women who don't share my enthusiasm for the project. I'm just getting started, however, and am nowhere ready to give up."

I sat back in my chair. "I realize projects such as the one you're proposing have been built over the ocean in a variety of locations around the world, but the wetlands on this island are environmentally sensitive, and there are a lot of laws that have been put into place to protect them."

"I'm not looking to destroy them. My goal is simply to create a place where visitors can fully enjoy them. I realize there are those who don't think I'll get my project off the ground, but between you and me, I have a much better chance at getting the permits than you might think."

I sat forward again and looked him in the eye. "And why is that?"

"Let's just say I have something to offer the island council in exchange that they desperately want."

"You're planning to bribe the council?"

King stood up. "It was nice meeting you. I think this interview is over."

I had to hand it to him, I thought, as I watched him walk away. His last statement had certainly captured my attention.

Chapter 3

When Jack had said he'd have food brought in, I was thinking Chinese or pizza. What he did was have one of the island's higher-end restaurants prepare and deliver a virtual feast that included prime rib, garlic mashed potatoes, buttery asparagus, farm-fresh salad, and a chocolate concoction for dessert. Not only was the food delicious but Jack served his best wine. The talk around the table centered on the possibility of conducting all our brainstorming sessions at Jack's.

"I spoke to Brit," I started in, once everyone was seated at the table. "She's going to check in with Abby this evening, and she's very excited we have a trail to follow."

"I'd be careful about getting the young widow's hopes up," Rick warned as he helped himself to a generous portion of creamy mashed potatoes. "All we really have is a theory, and a pretty wild one at that. If there's one thing I've learned after years of chasing ideas, it's that most theories don't work out."

"I guess that's true," I acknowledged as I stabbed a small slice of prime rib with my fork. "I just want Abby to know we're taking this seriously. I can't imagine having four children between three and ten to raise as well as a baby on the way. The poor woman must be frantic."

"Why exactly is Abby raising her sister's children?" Quinten asked after passing the asparagus to his left.

I took a roll and passed the basket before answering. "Her sister and her sister's husband were killed in an auto accident two years ago, leaving behind one-year-old twins, a five-year-old, and an eight-year-old. Timmy and Tommy are three now, Rebecca is seven, and Rachael is ten."

"That's a lot of responsibility for someone so young," Vikki commented as she moved her salad around on her plate. I'd noticed her appetite seemed to have disappeared as of late, and it was beginning to worry me. Perhaps I'd try to speak to her about it tomorrow.

For now, I let my concern go and answered the question. "Abby was her sister Tammy's only family. Their parents died when Tammy was twenty-two and Abby was seventeen. According to Brit, the sisters were very close, so even though Abby was only twenty-three at the time of her sister's death, she happily took on guardianship for all four children."

"Talk about an abrupt disruption to your life. The thought of someday having one child terrifies me, but to instantly become a mother to four grieving children..." Vikki said. "I can't even imagine."

"I'm sure it's been very difficult not just in terms of emotional stress but in the financial drain four kids must have on a young couple. When Brit and I spoke earlier, she told me that prior to her sister's death, Abby was a preschool teacher. Once the children came to live with them, Abby quit her job to be home with the kids and Bobby took on a second job, working on a fishing boat on his days off. Based on what Brit said, he worked almost every waking minute just to stay on top of things."

"My heart goes out to her," Quinten said. "I can't imagine what she must be going through. I felt as if my life was over when my wife passed, and I didn't have the extra burden of caring for children or trying to make ends meet."

I saw Gertie put her hand over Quinten's and give it a squeeze. At first glance, the quiet, sophisticated, and well-educated man and the loud, at times abrasive high-school dropout didn't appear to be an ideal pairing. But in the past couple of months, I'd been around the couple enough to realize that below the surface, they seemed to be exactly what the other one needed.

"Brit said Bobby worked part time on a couple of different boats so he'd have income every day," I informed the others after a short pause.

"So I guess Bobby probably knew the man whose boat burned," Quinten replied.

I glanced at Rick. He nodded, then filled us in. "Prior to the boat being dry-docked for repairs, Bobby occasionally signed on with Pop Seaton. Pop has lived in the area for a long time. Based on the information I managed to dig up during my investigation, Pop had been struggling financially. He had an old boat that needed a lot of repairs, and his competition had increased dramatically when a couple of new companies with better equipment started fishing in the area."

"Which supports the idea of him burning or having someone else burn his boat to collect the insurance," I said.

Rick took a small bite of his meat, then nodded. "The idea that Pop was after the insurance money did occur to me. The fire that destroyed his boat was the first that occurred, and I viewed it as an isolated event. I spoke with him, and he assured me that he was visiting friends and nowhere near the boat when it went up in flames. His alibi checked out, so I moved on to other suspects."

Vikki set down her fork and leaned back in her chair, abandoning all pretense that she was eating. She tucked a lock of her long blond hair behind one ear before asking the question I'd been pondering. "What's going on with Pop now? Is he still in the area?"

"He is," Rick confirmed. "He was able to purchase a used but much newer and better-equipped boat and is back on the water. I hear he's doing really well for himself."

"And the others?" Vikki asked. "Are they better off as well?"

"It would seem they are," Rick confirmed, "but I think for the purposes of this discussion, we should focus on one victim at a time."

Everyone agreed to Rick's plan. I noticed him frown, taking in the fact that Vikki hadn't eaten more than a couple of bites of salad. Was something going on I didn't know about? Vikki was my best friend. If her loss of appetite was due to a physical or emotional problem, I should know about it. I wanted to pull her aside, but this wasn't the right time. Instead, I said, "Jack has a whiteboard in his office. If someone will grab it once we're done eating, I'll take notes as we go through the cases. Maybe when we get everything written down, we'll start to see links between the victims that might not otherwise be evident."

The others agreed, and we finished our meal, and Jack went to get the board. I started clearing the dishes, and Vikki and Gertie joined me. By the time Jack returned, the dishes had been stacked and the leftovers put away. Everyone assumed Rick would run the brainstorming session, so when the whiteboard was set up and I had dry-erase markers in hand, I looked to the sofa where Rick and Vikki were seated.

He pulled out a file, looked it over quickly, then began to summarize. "On May 26 at approximately ten-fifteen p.m., the 911 operator received an anonymous call from a male, stating there was smoke coming from the center of the boatyard on the south side of the island. The fire crew responded and found Pop Seaton's boat, which had been dry-docked for repairs, completely engulfed in flames. The fire was burning so hot that by the time the firemen were able to control the flames, all that was left were the ashes from the wooden hull and twisted metal from the engine and fishing equipment. After he completed his investigation, the fire marshal determined that an accelerant had been used to ensure that the fire burned hot and fast. He further concluded that there were multiple ignition points. There seemed little doubt arson was responsible for the fire."

I noted the date and the basic facts on the board.

"At the time," Rick continued, "as I previously mentioned, I was investigating the fire in isolation. I learned the boat was not only insured but that the policy compensated the owner for the value of the boat and provided for replacement of a comparable size and use. I was certain the owner had set the fire to collect the insurance money. When I found out Pop's policy also compensated him for loss of income during the entire time he didn't have a boat to use, I was more certain than ever I had my motive and my arsonist."

"But it wasn't him," I said, remembering Pop had been away at the time of the fire.

"It didn't appear so. Still, something felt off to me."

"What do you mean?" Jack asked.

"For one thing, the insurance policy was hugely expensive. I knew Pop had been suffering some financial setbacks and couldn't imagine why he would spend a large amount of money to insure a boat that was on its last legs. When I found out it had been in dry dock for quite some time while he tried to come up with the money for the repairs, I was even more certain insurance fraud was behind the fire. Pop had an alibi, but I couldn't let go of the idea that he'd found a way to appear to be visiting friends up north while he was actually setting fire to his boat."

Rick paused, took a sip of water, and continued. "At about the time I'd decided to bring Pop in and attempt to force a confession out of him, I learned another fire had been called in to 911. This one was reported at approximately two-thirty a.m. on June 7. I was called at home, and by the time I responded, I found Jasper Wells's barn burned to the ground."

"Another well-insured piece of property?" Quinten, who had not been part of the Mastermind meeting, asked.

Rick nodded. "Not only was the barn well insured, it had been undergoing its own renovation and was empty of animals. The fire marshal was able to establish that an accelerant had been used this time too. By this point the theory I was working off was that one arsonist was responsible for both fires, despite the fact that there were a few differences between the two events."

"What sort of differences?" I asked.

"While an accelerant had been used in both fires, the type was different. Additionally, the ignition system used seemed to differ. Still, there were enough similarities to consider a single arsonist."

"It does sound like the same person was behind both fires, but why would anyone burn down these specific structures?" Quinten asked.

"I considered that the second fire had been used to draw attention away from the first one," Rick answered. "It was my belief that Pop knew I was on to him, so he threw another variable into the mix. The problem was, I couldn't find a single piece of evidence connecting Pop to either fire."

"Were both men insured through the same company?" Quinten asked.

"No," Rick answered. "Different companies based in different states."

"So the idea that the men may have burned each other's property for the insurance money hadn't occurred to you at that point?" Vikki asked.

"No. The idea hadn't occurred to me. Initially, I was certain the arsonist was Pop, but he seemed to have a hard alibi for the first fire and a soft one for the second. Eventually, I widened the scope of my investigation and considered a third player, some person who was linked to both Pop and Jasper. I wasn't making a lot of progress, but I consider the insurance payouts to be the motivator. I suspected both men paid a third player to set the fires in exchange for a payout."

I made a few notes on the whiteboard. "That's actually a solid theory."

"I thought so, but it was at that point that the third fire was called in on June 19 at four a.m. When I arrived at the bakeshop owned by Hillary Tisdale, it had already burned to the ground. As with the other two fires, an accelerant had been used, and as with the other structures, Ms. Tisdale's bakeshop was very well insured."

"Was she also out of town?" Vikki asked.

"She was at a baking conference she had signed up for six months before the fire. That made me take a closer look at my overall theory. When Pop and Jasper were the only victims, I assumed they had hired someone and planned the fires in advance. That would explain why they were conveniently out of town at the time of the fires. But with the addition of Hillary Tisdale to the mix, that theory didn't seem to stand up. I assumed whatever agreement the men had entered in to had been a recent development, but Hillary made plans to be out of town six months before the fire. It takes a lot of foresight to book a conference six months before you plan to engage in insurance fraud."

"Maybe Ms. Tisdale knew she would be gone and used the conference as an alibi for plans that were hatched after she'd made the reservation," I suggested.

"Maybe. The coincidences between the three cases were striking. All three fires were set on structures that were well insured, all three were burned after dark, all three were empty of people and animals, and all three owners were out of town when the fires occurred. I really felt like that meant something, I just didn't know what. I tried to find a link of some sort between the individuals but was unsuccessful. Finally, the fire marshal convinced me the arsonist was the link. He made a case that he or she was targeting specific properties that met certain criteria. That made sense. From then on, the investigation was less about the victims and more about identifying the arsonist."

Rick paused to take another drink, which allowed me to catch up a bit. It seemed there was a lot of information to capture for the board. Too much information.

"Who was next?" Vikki asked.

Rick offered her a gentle smile and then answered. "The next fire occurred just three days after Tisdale's bakeshop burned. Hannah Smith is a local artist who'd built an art studio in an unattached garage. The garage was burned to the ground, taking all the artwork with it, but the house was spared, and no one was injured. Like the three other fires, the building burned down late at night, and as with the others, an accelerant was used. By this point there was no doubt in anyone's mind we had a serial arsonist on our hands."

"Was Hannah insured as well?" I asked.

"She was. In fact, she had recently landed a spot in a huge New York art show, so she'd insured all her work at its maximum value."

"Too strange," I commented.

"Agreed," Rick said. "The similarities were so apparent that I knew there was a link. The question was, how did that link help us to identify the arsonist?"

"What about the fifth fire?" I asked. "The one where the man died."

"Two weeks after the art studio burned to the ground, fire number five was called in. Like the previous four, the fire was late at night, and an accelerant was used to ensure the structure would burn hot and fast. Like the others, the owner was out of town, but unlike them, there was a casualty. Apparently, a friend of the owner was staying in the house while he was away. The fire was intense; the poor guy never had a chance. A week after the man died, Bobby Boston was found dead in his garage with a suicide note that took responsibility for the fires. To be honest, it never set right with me that Bobby was the arsonist, but there were good arguments to be made for it."

"Such as?" I wondered.

"Such as the fact that as a firefighter, Bobby understood fire. He would have the knowledge needed to make ultimate use of the accelerant. Bobby's coworkers and friends were interviewed. Most couldn't believe he would do what he confessed to, but there were others who said he had been overly stressed with the added responsibility of his wife's nieces and nephews."

"None of that sounds like proof to me," I said.

"I agree." Rick stood up and began to pace. "In the end, what it came down to was that the sheriff wanted the case closed. He had a confession from a man who had the knowledge to do what he said he had, so he went with it."

Everyone sat in silence. Rick had provided us with a lot of information to take in. It seemed patterns existed beyond chance, but without a link they were pretty much useless. I didn't want to believe Abby's husband had set five fires before taking his own life, but I supposed I could understand why the sheriff would take the gift it seemed had been handed him in the form of a confession.

"The insurance thing is really bugging me," I said after a while. "Why would an insurance company write a policy with a value higher than the object they were insuring?"

"There are companies that will insure anything for the right price. Many times, the policies are for a short term, with a huge premium," Jack informed me.

I looked at Rick. "Were those policies all short term?"

"In the case of Pop's boat, no," Rick answered. "He first took out the policy when he bought the boat. It was a good policy that provided for full replacement, not just depreciated value and loss of income if the boat was rendered inoperable due to damage unrelated to normal wear and tear."

"Such as fire," I said.

"Exactly. Pop had been paying on the policy for years, but because it didn't cover normal wear and tear, he'd never filed a claim until the fire. I really thought he'd set the fire himself until everything else began to unfold."

"And the others?" Vikki asked.

"The bakeshop had just been purchased a year before and the policy Ms. Tisdale took out had been in place since that time. The barn had only been insured since the renovation began a few months before the fire. Mr. Wells indicated he'd invested a lot in materials and wanted to be sure they were covered in case of damage or theft."

"I guess that makes sense," I said.

"It did. On the surface, it appeared he only recovered what he'd lost, although he did end up with a brand-new barn instead of an old one with a facelift."

"And the artist?" Vikki asked.

"Ms. Smith seems to have come out on the winning end. She was an unknown artist who had only insured her work after being invited to take part in the art show. She may have managed to sell her art for the insured value. I guess we'll never know. If I remember correctly, she'd only had the policy for about a month, so she hadn't made any premium payments other than the deposit."

In a way, it sounded like other than Pop, Ms. Smith had gained the most from the arson spree. "And the house where the man died?" I asked.

"The policy was taken out when the house was purchased two years before the fire. It was standard, covering replacement value for the structure and contents. While the homeowner didn't exactly hit the lottery, the house needed a lot of repair he had put off, so one could argue that having a brand-new home to replace the old one could be considered a benefit."

"So, while everyone benefited to an extent from the fires, some of the victims came out further ahead, and some of the victims had a lot invested in the policy, while others didn't," Jack summarized.

"Exactly."

"What are we thinkin'?" Gertie asked, speaking up for the first time since our brainstorming session had begun.

We all looked at one another. *The Strangers on a Train* idea had seemed reasonable until we started the discussion, but now? Now, I couldn't imagine five people had all somehow met and come up with such a convoluted plan.

"Perhaps we should define what we're trying to do," Quinten suggested.

I scrunched up my face. "I don't understand what you mean."

"Are we trying to identify the person or persons who set fire to the five structures, or are we trying to prove Bobby Boston didn't commit suicide?"

"Aren't the two questions basically the same thing?" Vikki asked.

"No, Quinten is right," I jumped in. "There are several things going on here that may or may not be related. Identifying the arsonist would be a by-product of our desire to help Abby in proving her husband didn't kill himself."

"Don't we have to find the real arsonist before we can prove Bobby is innocent?" Vikki reasoned.

"It doesn't matter whether he set the fires. At least not if our main goal is to help Abby. All we have to prove is that he was murdered for whatever reason."

The room fell silent. I supposed everyone was trying to wrap their head around the point Quinten had been trying to make."

"Would you be willing to look at Bobby's autopsy report?" I asked Quinten.

"Sure," he answered. "If you can get a copy."

I turned to look at Rick. "Can you do that?"

"I can."

I clapped my hands together. "Okay, then. Let's start there. If we can prove Bobby was murdered, Abby should be able to collect the insurance money whether we figure out the rest of the mystery or not."

"But we're still goin' to work on the arsons?" Gertie asked.

I shrugged. "Sure. I know I'm curious about them. But getting Abby the money she needs to raise those five kids is our first priority. Agreed?"

Everyone nodded.

"Fantastic," I said. "Quinten and Rick can get together tomorrow. In the meantime, we can all follow up on any leads we have. The Mastermind group is meeting tomorrow, so if we decide we need help, we can assign tasks for everyone to take care of." I looked at Gertie and Quinten. "You're both invited to the meeting. We're having dinner at six and meeting directly after." I glanced at Rick. "I know you don't normally attend, but it could be important this time."

He hesitated.

"It's for Abby and her kids."

"Okay. But I'll be there as Vikki's boyfriend, not in any sort of official capacity."

"Perfect." I glanced around the room. "Who's up for dessert?"

Chapter 4

Wednesday, January 24

When I went downstairs the next morning, Vikki was sitting at the kitchen table nursing a cup of tea. Jack and I had decided I should bring Kizzy home with me last night because his mother was coming today, and he wanted to have time to eradicate every trace of dog hair from the house. My first order of business, I realized, was to take Kizzy out for her morning constitutional. When I returned to the house several minutes later, Vikki was still sitting alone at the table. I fed the happy, energetic puppy, then made my own cup of tea.

I blew on it, waiting for it to cool. "It looks like we might get rain today."

"I heard we're in for a couple of inches."

"Personally, I could do without it. Between keeping an eye on the puppy tornado, writing my article on the proposed development that would bring huts to the marsh, and getting everything ready for our dinner tonight, I'm not in the mood to spend the whole day making mad dashes from one place to another."

"Yeah."

I paused as I studied Vikki's face. She was as beautiful as ever, but she looked tired. "Is everything okay?" I asked.

"I'm fine."

"You look sort of run-down. Are you sleeping okay?"

Vikki nodded, then stood up. "I have a conference call with my agent. I should head back to my cabin. I'll see you tonight."

I watched as she stood up and walked out the door. I was sure she wasn't feeling well, but if that were true, why had she come over here in the first place? We'd established a pattern of meeting in the kitchen of the main house for breakfast despite her moving into her own cabin, but if one of us wasn't feeling well, or if we'd spent the night elsewhere or had a guest of the opposite sex to entertain in the morning, we skipped it. If Vikki hadn't been feeling well, all she needed to do was text.

Maybe I should ask Rick if he knew what was going on. Of course, even if he did, he wouldn't tell me if Vikki had told him not to. No, I needed to get it directly from the horse's mouth, but Vikki didn't seem to be in a sharing mood. She and I usually told each other everything. It concerned me that she was shutting me out of whatever was wrong. If she didn't seem better by tomorrow, I'd have to force the issue.

"Are you done with your breakfast?" I asked Kizzy, who'd come into the kitchen and plopped down in front of the wood-burning fireplace.

It looked like Vikki wasn't the only one having a hard time getting going this morning. I glanced at the clock and decided to make some cinnamon rolls. Garrett loved them, and I'd found since I'd brought him home I would do almost anything to add some happiness to his otherwise difficult day. Once the rolls were in the oven, I put on a pot of coffee.

"Do I smell cinnamon?" Garrett asked a while later as he wheeled himself into the kitchen with Blackbeard, his parrot, on his shoulder. We'd remodeled the house so he could easily access any room on the first floor with his wheelchair. I couldn't imagine being stuck in a chair all day, but he seemed to be making the best of it. He usually had a smile on his face, and his sunny disposition brightened even the gloomiest days.

"You do smell cinnamon. I have rolls in the oven. They'll be ready in about ten minutes. Coffee?"

"Please." Garrett rolled across the room and set Blackbeard onto his perch. The bird had talked almost nonstop when Garrett was away, but since he'd been back, he barely spoke at all. At least not to me. I did hear them chatting from time to time, and they enjoyed watching television together. I was concerned about Blackbeard's health, but Jack thought he was less of a chatterbox now because he was happier and more relaxed with Garrett home.

"How'd your brainstorming session go last night?" he asked after I set his cup in front of him.

I filled Garrett in on the highlights while we both sipped our coffee and waited for the rolls to be done.

Garrett wasn't a writer, but he'd lived on Gull Island his entire life and had insight on local matters that had helped us out in the past.

"I remember that young husband of Abby's," Garrett said. "He used to come by the senior home when I was living there to visit a man whose life he had saved in a fire. I didn't know him well, but he seemed to be a nice and caring man. Not at all the sort to start fires or leave a wife to raise a houseful of kids on her own."

"That's the impression I have of him based on what I've heard. I really hope we can help Abby. It breaks my heart that she's going through so much on her own."

"She's not alone. She has you and Brit and the others on her side. Seems to me she's in pretty good hands."

I hoped Garrett was right.

The timer dinged on the oven and I got up to get the rolls just as Clara came down from her second-story room, followed by her cat, Agatha, who hissed at Kizzy. The pup didn't lift her head in response, but she did thump her tail as Agatha strolled past the rug she was lying on in search of her own breakfast.

"We should call George," Clara said. "You know how he loves cinnamon rolls."

"Good idea," Garrett said, and he picked up his cell and dialed George's number.

Clara crossed the room and picked up an old quilt that she wrapped around her shoulders before taking a seat at the table.

"Are you cold? I can turn up the heat," I offered.

"I'm not cold, but I do have a chill."

"A chill?"

"Trouble is coming."

I set a plate of rolls on the table, as well as four plates and forks. "There's a storm on the way. That's probably what you're sensing. Vikki said we're supposed to get a couple of inches of rain."

"Vikki was here?" Garrett asked.

"She was, but she left shortly after I came down. It looked like she didn't feel well, although she said she was fine."

I decided to add a bowl of fruit to the table, as well as a pitcher of orange juice. I loved sweets for breakfast as much as the next person, but I usually tried to eat an apple or orange too.

"Good morning, everyone." George came through the kitchen door from the patio. "Looks like we're in for some weather."

"According to Vikki, a couple of inches," I said. "Coffee?"

"Please." George bent down to pet Kizzy and offer her a treat before taking a seat next to Clara. "I know Clara is the resident psychic, but you must have read my mind," George said to me. "I woke up thinking about hot, gooey cinnamon rolls."

"Maybe Clara is rubbing off on me," I said as I refilled everyone's cup.

"How was your brainstorming session last night?" George asked.

I repeated what I'd just told Garrett so that everyone was on the same page.

"Quinten had a good point about narrowing in on what you're trying to accomplish," George said. "It's easy to get bogged down in the facts. Before you know it, you've left your primary objective behind and are off chasing rainbows."

"Sounds like you've had some experience in that area."

George nodded at me. "I had a serious case of wandering attention span when I was younger. In fact, I almost didn't complete my doctoral thesis on time after I stumbled across an interesting side note that had nothing to do with the paper I was writing but had somehow managed to capture my imagination."

I glanced at George over the top of my cup. "I assume you did finish."

"Yes, but only after my adviser whipped some sense into me and got me back on track."

"Seems to me you're still prone to wander at times, my old friend." Garrett chuckled.

"I'll admit as much." George laughed too. "While indulging in an unplanned side trip on a tight deadline isn't the best idea, I've found that in life, as in writing, it's the unexpected side trip that makes all the difference."

As a wannabe novelist, I loved to chat with George. He had these little tips he never presented as advice that turned out to be very helpful. I loved the imagery of unexpected deviations bringing clarity and variation into your life. Vikki, who was a much more accomplished author than I could ever hope to be, had told me many times that if you allowed your characters freedom to choose their own path, you'd often stumble across just what you needed at the exact moment you needed it.

The four of us spent the next hour chatting. There were days when I wanted nothing more than to sit and chat with these interesting, stimulating people, but I had an article to write, a dinner to plan, and some follow-up to do on ideas I'd had after last night's brainstorming. I excused myself and headed upstairs to get ready to start the day.

When I came back downstairs, the kitchen group had broken up, and I sat down to make a grocery list. I'd need to stop by the market while I was out to pick up the items I'd need for dinner that evening. It was a cool day and I wasn't going to be in the store long, so I decided to bring Kizzy along with me. I found I rather enjoyed having a furry companion as I did my errands. Who knew that Jillian Hanson, who until recently had been a lifelong apartment dweller, enjoyed spending time with a dog?

By the time I parked in front of the only full-service market on the island, it had begun to rain lightly. I gave Kizzy a toy and told her to be a good girl while I ran inside. I'd decided to make a pot of chowder for dinner, so I headed to the seafood aisle to see what had been brought in fresh today.

"Morning, Luke," I said to the butcher.

"Jill. What can I help you with?"

"I want to make a seafood chowder." I picked up a couple of packages of shrimp, which I tossed into my basket, along with a couple of lobster tails and some scallops.

"I have some crab in the back that was just delivered this morning."

Adding crab to the chowder might be too much seafood, but adding it to the top of a salad sounded delicious. "Okay, I'll take a couple if you'll clean them for me."

"Not a problem. Give me a few minutes."

"I have to grab some other things. I'll be back when I'm done."

I headed around the perimeter of the store, picking up fresh produce and dairy products. I chose some freshly baked bread from the bakery, which was where I found Brooke Johnson, an elementary schoolteacher as well as the volunteer coordinator for many island events.

She greeted me with a smile. "I was just thinking about you."

If Brooke was thinking about you, that most likely meant she needed your help with one of her projects. "Let me guess: you're recruiting volunteers for the Valentine's Day dance."

"Actually, no. I am, however, looking for help for the Spring Fling in April. I hoped you could participate on the planning committee and provide some free publicity in the newspaper in the form of a series of articles about the event."

"That sounds like something I can do. When do you want to start?"

Brooke tossed two loaves of bread into her basket while I began sorting through the French loaves.

"The first meeting of the planning committee is on Wednesday next week. We're thinking of meeting in the library, but I'll let you know if that changes. As far as the articles, I thought we could focus on different aspects of the event. I'd like to get started in a few weeks and maybe run one every other week."

I held one of the freshly baked loaves up to my nose before tossing it into my basket. "Okay. Why don't you give me a rough outline of what you want the articles to look like, then we can meet to discuss the specifics. This will be my first spring on Gull Island, so you'll have to help me with the details."

Brooke hugged me. "Perfect. I knew you'd help. You're always so generous with your time."

"I try to help out when I can." I grabbed a package of fresh bagels for tomorrow's breakfast.

"Abby Boston told me that you're trying to help her get the insurance money she has coming to her. I told her if anyone could find the truth behind her husband's death, it would be you."

"I hope your faith in me isn't misplaced. It's a complicated situation."

Brooke leaned a hip against her basket. "I know. And I know you'll do what you can. I feel so bad for the poor thing. I don't know Abby well, but her nieces attend the school where I teach, so she joined the PTA. I'm the teacher rep, so we've worked on a couple of projects together."

"Do you know if she has any close friends? Someone she might talk to about personal matters?"

Brooke tilted her head, allowing her long blond hair to fall to one side. "I know she's friends with Laurie Olson. Laurie has really been there for her since Bobby died, helping with babysitting and carpooling. If Abby were to share her feelings with anyone, it would be her." Brooke paused and then added, "You know what we should do? We should throw Abby a baby shower. Her sister's children were past the infant stage when they came to live with her, so I bet she doesn't have anything for a newborn."

"That's a great idea. I'd love to help you plan something if you're willing to take the lead."

"Fantastic. Maybe we can do lunch on Friday to discuss both the shower and the Spring Fling. We have a half day at school then, so I'd be able to meet by one."

"I'd like that. Gertie's?"

"That would be perfect." Brooke glanced at her watch. "I need to get a move on or I'll be late for my afternoon classes."

"Before you go, can you tell me how I can get hold of Laurie Olson?"

"She works at the new fitness center in town. She should be there this morning, if you want to stop by."

Brooke hurried off and I returned to the meat and seafood counter to pick up my crab. I didn't want to leave the fresh food in the car for too long, so I decided to drop off both the groceries and the puppy at the house before heading to the center of town, where the fitness center was located.

******

Fit and Fabulous focused on female clients. I'd been thinking about checking it out ever since it opened, but so far, I hadn't found the time. The facility was located along one of the main thoroughfares downtown, and parking could be found in a public lot across the street. By the time I got there, the rain had intensified, so I pulled my jacket over my head and made a run for it.

"Welcome to Fit and Fabulous," a cheery young woman who looked to have zero percent body fat greeted me. "Are you a member?"

"No. I'm not here to work out. I hoped to speak to Laurie Olson, if she's available."

"Laurie's teaching a spin class. She should be free in about ten minutes if you'd like to wait."

"Yeah, okay, that would be fine," I said.

"Would you like a tour while you wait?" the young woman asked. "We're running a special for the entire month of January."

I glanced around at the clean, brightly lit lobby. When I lived in New York, I walked everywhere, but since I'd been on the island, I'd traded that for driving. I really could use some exercise. "I'd love a tour."

She grinned. "Fantastic. I'll have Anton show you around."

Let me start off by telling you that Anton was not only fit and muscular, he had a sharp face with chiseled features that made me think of a Greek god. If Anton was the bait provided to overweight and stressed women, Fit and Fabulous was going to be a huge success.

I tried not to stare at my gorgeous tour guide as he showed me the weight room, the yoga room, the Pilates room, and the aerobics equipment. The facility was pretty awesome, with up-to-date equipment, certified instructors, a fantastic locker room complete with a sauna, and even a small lap pool. I hadn't intended to sign a one-year contract when I arrived, but by the time Laurie was free to talk, that was what I'd done.

"Are you Jill Hanford?" asked a petite woman in a tight-fitting sweat suit.

"I am. Are you Laurie?"

She nodded. "How can I help you?"

"I wanted to speak with you about a project I'm helping Abby Boston with, if you have a few minutes."

"You're Brit's friend."

I nodded. "Do you know Brit?"

73

"Sure. She was one of our first clients. She told me that her group was going to try to help Abby get her money." Laurie tossed the towel that had been wrapped around her neck into a large hamper. "There's a juice lounge in the back. We can talk there."

Fit and Fabulous was pretty awesome for a small community like Gull Island. I wouldn't have guessed there were enough fitness-inclined women here to keep the facility in business, but the place was packed.

"Would you like some juice?" Laurie asked as we entered the lounge.

"Thank you, but I only have a few minutes and I don't want to take up more of your time than necessary. If you could just answer a few questions for me, that would be very helpful."

Laurie indicated that I should take a seat at one of the tables and she sat down across from me. "What do you want to know?"

I took a moment to gather my thoughts. "I guess Abby told you that Brit asked our group to help her prove her husband was murdered."

She nodded.

"What I'm most interested in at this point is your overall impression of Bobby, particularly at the time he died."

"Impression?" Laura asked.

"How he seemed emotionally. Was he happy and energetic? Did he seem stressed and withdrawn? Was there something going on in his life that was worrying him?"

Laurie answered carefully. "I first met Abby and Bobby four years ago, shortly after they moved to the island. We lived in the same apartment building at the time, and they had a lot in common with me and my boyfriend. We started getting together for dinner and going out on double dates. After I broke up with the man I'd been seeing, the three of us remained friends."

I watched Laurie's face as she spoke. She appeared to be both sad and hesitant. I decided to remain silent and let her set the pace for our conversation.

"Then Abby's sister died a couple of years ago," Laurie continued. "It was such a hard time for Abby. Not only did she lose the sister she adored but she was given custody of four young children. The twins were only one and didn't really get what was going on, but the girls were older and understandably grief-stricken." Laurie's eyes narrowed. "I don't know how Abby and Bobby got through it, but somehow they did. Abby quit her job to be a full-time mom and Bobby took on a bunch of side jobs to help make up for the loss of income. Somehow, they bought a house large enough for the six of them, and by the time Abby found out she was pregnant, the new family had settled into what looked like a comfortable routine."

"It sounds as if Abby's pregnancy wasn't planned."

"No, it wasn't. Abby was totally freaked out when she found out about the baby. Poor Bobby was already working every waking hour. She couldn't see how they were going to pay the medical bills and buy the things they'd need for a newborn. I could see Abby's pregnancy put stress on their relationship. Neither of them had the emotional strength to carry another burden, and I'm afraid, at the time, that's what they considered the baby: a burden."

Laurie was quiet for a moment, and I once again elected not to speak. I figured I could ask questions later if I needed more details or clarification.

"Anyway, life in the Boston household had grown increasingly tense, but my overall impression was that Abby and Bobby loved each other and would find a way to work things out. If he'd lived, I know in my heart he would have loved that baby as much as Abby will."

"I'm sure he would have. An unexpected pregnancy can be difficult to deal with even if you don't already have four children to raise. The financial hardship alone must have seemed overwhelming."

"It did. And to add to everything else, there was a rumor going around that there were going to be layoffs at the firehouse. Bobby was the last to be hired, so he assumed he'd be the first to be laid off. The arson spree started up at about that time, so the layoffs were put on hold."

"So, if the arsonist hadn't come onto the scene, Bobby would most likely have been out of a job?"

"That's the way I understood it," Laurie answered. "I think Bobby and one other firefighter were targeted for layoffs."

Oh boy; that didn't sound good. I seemed to have discovered a motive for Bobby to have set the fires. I closed my eyes and stifled a groan.

"Are you okay?" Laurie asked.

"I'm fine. Back to the story. Do you think it's possible Bobby had become so overwhelmed with the pressure of an unwanted pregnancy, raising four kids who weren't his own, and possible unemployment that he could have taken his own life?"

Laurie shook her head. "No way. Bobby was going through a tough time, but he loved Abby. He would never have left her to fend for herself."

We spoke for a few more minutes, but then Laurie had to go teach a yoga class. I thanked her and went out into the rain to my car with a feeling of dread that things might not work out the way we all hoped they would. If you looked at the totality of the stressors weighing Bobby Boston down at the time of his death, it seemed totally believable that he'd snapped and done exactly what the note said he had.

Chapter 5

I left Fit and Fabulous and sat in the car for a moment, considering what to do next. I needed to write the article about the goofy condo project, which, as far as I was concerned, had virtually no chance of getting past the island council, but before I could do that, I needed a bit more information. I decided to stop at Betty Boop's Beauty Salon to see if Mayor Betty Sue Bell was available to chat. Betty Sue was an interesting character I'd found to be quite helpful when it came to understanding the political climate of our community.

Betty Boop's was decorated in a fifties' motif. Not only did the décor take you back in time as soon as you walked in the front door, the hairdressers who worked there, including the mayor herself, dressed the part, with big hair and heavy makeup.

"Morning, Betty Sue," I greeted as I entered from the rain-drenched sidewalk.

"My, don't you look like a drowned rat?"

I put my hand to my hair. I supposed I did look a fright after spending the morning running from my car to one place or another in the pouring rain. "I guess this isn't the best day to be running errands, but I'm on deadline and wondered if we could chat about the huts Derek King wants to build."

"Come on in and sit a spell. It's been dead this morning. Not that I blame folks for not wanting to venture out in this storm just to have their roots touched up." Betty Sue motioned for me to have a seat in the waiting area. "How can I help you?"

"I met with King yesterday, so I have a general idea of what he has in mind. Call me crazy, but the idea seems nuts to me. Is there any chance at all he'll pull this thing off?"

Betty Sue crossed her arms over her ample chest. Her long, hot-pink nails reflected off the light from the overhead lamps. She pursed her thick lips, which she'd painted with a pink as bright as her nails, then tilted her head just a tad to the left before she answered. "The project King is proposing isn't at all compatible with the regulations we've adopted over the years to protect the ecology of the marsh area. When he first brought the idea to the council, I, like you, thought he had a screw loose. Since that first meeting, however, I've come to understand that he's a shrewd and cunning businessman."

"How so?"

"For one thing, he's set up a series of contingencies that, when taken as a whole, have a domino effect."

"Can you elaborate?"

Betty Sue, who was standing next to her hairdresser's chair, leaned a hip against it. "King is proposing to build these raised condos over marshland owned by the Littleton trust. From what I understand, he's offering a ridiculous amount of money for what's otherwise useless land. He's built a contingency into his offer that the sale will only proceed if he receives the permits he's seeking to build his project."

"And I take it the Littleton family wants to sell the land?"

"They do. Marcus Littleton was a rich man who amassed quite a fortune in his lifetime. At one point, he owned most of the land on this island. But it seems his descendants aren't as industrious. The estate, which was once valued in the billions, has been whittled down to a fortune so small that referring to it as one seems grandiose. Over the years, the family has sold off one piece of land after another. Now, there are very few acres of any value left to sell."

"So the family is motivated to sell the worthless marshland they own to a developer. What does the island council have to say?"

"As you may have heard, the council has been looking in to building a facility to convert and store solar energy to be used as a backup to the island's current power source. It's an ambitious idea that will only produce a fraction of the energy the island needs, but with all the power outages we've been having, it has strong backing."

"Sounds expensive."

"It will be," Betty Sue confirmed. "A couple of the council members got together and found a grant that will help us buy the equipment we need, including the very expensive batteries required for such a venture, but the grant doesn't cover either the purchase of the property or the construction of the building. There's a proposal floating around that a small increase in the sales tax could cover the cost of the building, but a piece of land large enough for such a facility will still be needed. As it turns out, the Littletons just happen to own the perfect property. They're willing to sell it to the town for a very reasonable amount, but only if King's project is approved."

"Yikes."

"Yikes is right. What should be a very simple decision has turned into something very complex. There's a subcommittee studying the situation, but I don't see a decision coming down soon. But it seems Mr. King is a patient man and willing to wait."

I sat back in my chair. "I'm new around here and haven't had to live through what I understand can be extensive power outages, but agreeing to the condo project for any reason seems unwise. I almost feel as if it could set a precedent."

"Perhaps. All I can really say is that the issue isn't as cut and dried as you might think."

I thanked Betty Sue for taking the time to explain things to me and then headed to the newspaper. I wasn't sure if Jack was coming in today with his mother due to arrive, but I figured it wouldn't be a bad idea to check on things. The contractors who'd been working in the conference room yesterday had completed that part of the project, and as far as I knew, Jack had put a halt to further construction during his mother's stay.

"So you *are* here," I greeted him as I entered the office. "I wasn't sure you were coming in today."

Jack glanced up but didn't respond.

"Is she here?"

"She is."

I hung up my jacket and set my purse on the desk. "How's it going?"

"Given the fact that I'm a grown man who basically ran away from home and is currently hiding from his mother, not so good."

I grimaced. "That bad, huh?"

Jack nodded before returning his attention to his computer screen. I could see he was in a delicate mood, and if I was smart, that would indicate I should leave him to his thoughts. But when it comes to human interactions, I'm not always the best at taking my own advice.

"She does understand that this is your life and your career and therefore all decisions regarding both are yours to make?"

"It's complicated."

"Complicated how?"

"Just complicated." Jack looked up at me. "Did you want something?"

I hesitated. "No. I just came by to check in before I went back to the resort to write my article."

"Okay, then." He returned his attention to his computer, effectively shutting me out.

I wanted to point out that being rude to me wasn't going to help him with his problems with his mother, but instead, I grabbed my things and stormed out. If Jack didn't want my company, that was fine. I didn't have time for his drama anyway.

******

"Who stole your puppy?" Brit asked later that afternoon while I was making the seafood chowder.

I glanced at Kizzy, who was sleeping by the fire in plain sight, so I assumed she meant the question in a figurative sense, in relation to the amount of banging around I was doing, and not literally.

"Jack irritated me, and I guess I'm taking out my frustrations on the pots and pans," I explained. "I'm sorry. I'll try to finish the soup without all the noise."

Brit shrugged. "It's not bothering me, but isn't this the time of day Garrett usually takes a nap?"

I gently placed the knife I was holding on the counter. "You're right. I wasn't even thinking about how annoying all the racket was to everyone around me."

"Care to tell me what the problem is?" Brit grabbed an apple from the bowl on the table and took a bite.

"Jack's mom is in town."

"And that made you mad?"

"Jack and his mom are fighting, which, given the circumstances, I understand. But when I stopped by the newspaper today and tried to talk to him about it, he snapped at me. His mom is the controlling, dictator type, and she's making him miserable. I don't know why he snapped at me for trying to help."

Brit hopped up onto the counter, continuing to eat her apple while we chatted. "I'd be willing to bet if Jack's mother has him on edge, he'd be likely to snap at anyone who tried to get involved."

"I wasn't *getting involved*. I was trying to help," I reasoned.

"Remember when that friend of yours from New York offered you that job last month?"

"Yeah. What does that have to do with this?" I asked.

"Remember how when your ex came to town to try to convince you to take the offer, you felt all pressured and flustered?"

"Yeah. So?"

"Do you remember what Jack did?"

My shoulders dropped as the reality of what Brit was trying to tell me finally sank in. "He supported me, while giving me the space I needed to make up my mind."

Brit raised a perfectly shaped brow.

"I guess I owe Jack an apology."

Brit hopped off the counter and crossed the room to toss the apple core in the trash. "You probably do, but I wouldn't do it now. I'm sure his relationship with his mother is complicated. The best way to support him is to give him the space he needs to figure out whatever he needs to do."

"Thanks, Brit. I guess I needed to hear that."

She shrugged. "My door is always open."

Brit was more than a decade younger than me, but at times she demonstrated an emotional maturity I was still working to achieve.

"I spoke to Abby's friend Laurie today," I said.

Brit turned toward me. "And…?"

"And I think we should discuss something she said."

"Okay," Brit said with a tone of trepidation. She slipped onto one of the barstools. "What's up?"

"Laurie told me that prior to the fires, the firehouse where Bobby worked was looking at layoffs."

Brit let out a breath. "You think Bobby started the fires to save his job?"

"He was under a lot of pressure financially, raising four children that weren't even his, with a baby of his own on the way. Add the threat of a layoff to the mix and you have a cocktail that would cause a lot of people to snap."

Brit didn't respond right away, but I could see she was thinking hard. We both wanted Bobby to be innocent of the deeds he seemed to have claimed in the suicide note, but now that we were starting to investigate, it seemed he might actually be guilty of setting the fires.

"Did Abby mention the layoffs to you?" I asked Brit.

"No. But she may not have known about them. Bobby might have kept the situation to himself to protect her from more stress."

I supposed that made sense.

"Did Laurie say anything else?" Brit asked. "Anything less damaging?"

"She did talk Bobby up. She admitted the relationship between the Bostons became strained after they found out they were expecting, but she felt they would have worked through it and been fine if Bobby hadn't died."

I watched Brit's face as she tried to process the information I provided. We both knew we needed to be honest about what we discovered with the group, and that it could change our opinion about whether Bobby had set the fires or killed himself.

"I really don't want to believe Bobby committed suicide."

I placed my hand on Brit's arm. "I know. The idea isn't sitting well with me either. The thing is, before I spoke to Laurie, one of my main arguments against the idea that Bobby was the arsonist was that he didn't seem to have a motive."

"And now he does."

"I'm sorry."

Brit normally wasn't the emotional sort, so it really tugged at my heart when I noticed a tear in the corner of her eye.

"Of course, having a motive doesn't make a man guilty," I added. "I'm fine with continuing the investigation, and I'm sure the rest of the group will be as well. We'll keep looking until we know the truth for sure."

Brit's smile was weak. "Thanks, Jill."

******

On a positive note, everyone loved my soup. On a less positive one, Jack didn't show up or even call to say he wasn't coming. I realized I probably shouldn't have stormed out of his office earlier, but I didn't think that would have a long-term effect on our relationship. I wanted to call him, but Brit had been right when she suggested I give him some space. I knew Jack cared about me, and I was fairly certain he wouldn't let this become a permanent barrier between us. Intellectually, I knew I should wait for him to be ready to talk, but emotionally, I was a wreck. I struggled with the need to act versus the need to wait all through dinner. By the time I served dessert, I'd settled on a compromise. I texted him to say I was sorry about the exchange we'd had that afternoon, and that I understood his need for space and should take the time he needed. I told him that I cared very deeply for him and would be here when he was ready to talk.

After I sent the text I returned to the kitchen, where I found Brit and Vikki, both looking as miserable as me.

I put my hand on Vikki's shoulder. "Are you okay?"

She nodded. "I'm just a little tired."

I knew whatever was going on was more than being tired but didn't push it. I turned my attention to Brit. "It'll be okay. Whatever happens, I'm committed to seeing this investigation through."

The three of us headed into the living room, where the rest of the group seemed happy and in high spirits.

"Are we ready to get started?" I asked.

"I think we are," George answered.

Everyone took a seat. I glanced at Quinten. "Perhaps we should hear what you have to say first. If you're ready, that is."

"I'm ready," Quinten said. Our meetings were informal, so everyone remained seated, even those of us who were speaking, except me because I'd volunteered to man the whiteboard again.

"I was able to have a look at Bobby Boston's autopsy report," Quinten began. "While reading a report written by someone else can in no way be compared to having the opportunity to look at the body, I can say that the attending medical examiner seemed to have done an adequate job." Quinten cleared his throat before he continued. "Bobby died from carbon monoxide poisoning. There were no visible defensive wounds on the body, and I didn't find reason to suspect foul play prior his getting into the automobile. The ME did find a very small bruise above Bobby's top lip, which could indicate that an agent such as chloroform had been used to knock him out before he was placed in the vehicle by someone else, but the evidence was far from conclusive."

"But it's possible," Brit said.

"Sure. It's possible. However, the crime scene unit was unable to find fingerprints, clothing or hair fibers, or anything that would support that theory. I believe if a suicide note hadn't been found, a more thorough investigation would have been conducted that may have turned up additional evidence. Or not."

"What about drugs or alcohol? Were either involved?" George asked.

"No. Bobby was drug and alcohol free at the time of his death."

"So we have nothing?" Brit asked.

Quinten paused.

"You have something?" Brit amended.

"I'm not sure," he admitted. "Mrs. Boston told the deputy who interviewed her that when she returned home from shopping she smelled exhaust and went into the garage. She saw her husband in the car and called out to him. When he didn't respond, she approached the vehicle. She realized her husband was unconscious and opened the driver's side door. She saw immediately it was too late to save him. She returned to the house and called 911. When asked if the car was running when she entered the garage, she said it wasn't."

Brit jumped up. "So who turned off the car? If Bobby was intent on killing himself, it makes no sense that he'd turn off the engine before he was dead. And after he was dead...well, it would have been impossible."

I looked at Rick. "Is that correct? Was the engine off?"

"According to the fire chief, who was first on the scene, the engine was off when he arrived and the exhaust in the enclosed area had dissipated considerably. The crime scene guys decided Mrs. Boston must have instinctively turned off the engine when she approached the car but had forgotten she had done so."

"That seems like a pretty big supposition to me," Brit challenged.

"Okay, wait." I held up my hands. "Didn't it occur to anyone that someone other than Bobby turned off the engine just moments before Abby came home?"

"It was discussed, but it seemed unlikely," Rick answered. "And don't forget, we had a suicide note. The note seemed to explain a lot and was taken pretty seriously."

"But Bobby had no motive to start those fires," Garrett spoke up.

I glanced at Brit. She nodded at me.

"Actually, he may have had motive." I really didn't want to say anything to cast additional doubt on Bobby's suicide, but if we were to figure things out, we needed to have all the cards on the table. "I spoke to Abby's best friend today. She told me that prior to the arson spree, the fire department was looking at laying off two men. Bobby was the most recent hire."

There was an audible groan in the room.

"That doesn't mean he started the fires," I pointed out. "It only means he had motive to create some business for his crew."

The room fell silent. After a moment, Brit said, "I know it looks bad, but I'm not willing to give up until we know for sure exactly what happened. Maybe Bobby is guilty of doing exactly what the note suggests he did, but maybe he's not. Abby deserves to know the truth."

"I agree." I sat forward. "Whatever we find out, good or bad, I'm in this until we know for certain."

"It does sort of feel like an uphill battle," Alex said.

"If you aren't man enough for the job, we can do this without you," Brit challenged.

"Settle down," Alex said. "I didn't say I wouldn't help. I was just pointing out that we have a tough job ahead of us."

"Well, I'm in until the end," Vikki said.

"And I'm in until the fat lady sings," Gertie seconded.

"Where Gertie goes, I go," Quinten said.

"Let's assign tasks," George suggested. "We can check in with Jill if we find anything significant and then meet back here on Monday for our regular meeting."

"I can talk to Abby again," Brit offered. "Maybe she knows more than she's shared so far."

"I'll go with you," I volunteered. "We'll go tomorrow."

"I know a couple of the guys at the firehouse. I'll talk to them to see what they know," Alex said.

"And I'll call a colleague to see if he can dig up some additional information that might not have been included in the autopsy report," Quinten said. "Sometimes minor details are noted but not transferred to the official form."

"I'll bring snacks to the next meeting." Gertie clapped her hands together, making her bracelets jingle.

Rick didn't volunteer to do anything, but he never did. Vikki usually offered to do something, but tonight she was quiet. It scared me that she looked so pale.

I turned my attention back to the group. "I wonder if we should speak to the fire victims. If they're truly just victims and not accomplices, they probably won't know anything, but I don't suppose it would hurt to strike up conversations to see what comes of it."

"I have time tomorrow," Brit informed me. "If you want, we can visit whoever we can track down after we talk to Abby."

"Okay. Does anyone else have anything?"

"Did anyone get Bobby's alibi for the time of the fires?" George asked. "I realize he was dead, so the investigator would be unable to ask him, but there are others who would know if he was at work or at home."

"Good question," Rick answered. "I'll check into it tomorrow."

Chapter 6

Thursday, January 25

Jack still hadn't called, or even returned my text, by the next morning. I understood he was dealing with some tough issues, but I thought our relationship meant enough to him that he would reach out in some small way to let me know things were okay between us. The fact that he hadn't terrified me. I wanted to try calling him but knew I should give it more time, as Brit had suggested. If he hadn't contacted me by the end of the day, I would take the initiative and call him.

In the meantime, Kizzy needed to go out despite the rain. The storm that had blown in hadn't been as intense as was first predicted, but it seemed it was going to linger longer than I'd hoped. After pulling on heavy jeans, a long-sleeved shirt, and a sweatshirt, I grabbed my tennis shoes and left the room. In the kitchen, I found George, Garrett, and Clara drinking coffee and discussing the latest news. I greeted them before pulling on my waterproof slicker and went out into the wet morning.

Walking along the beach on a wet, cool morning actually did a lot to improve my mood. There's something so relaxing about the waves as they roll on to the shore. Kizzy didn't seem to mind the light rain in the least and ran up and down the beach, chasing every bird brave enough to dare landing in her line of sight. Initially, I'd planned to make our outing a quick one, but the more I walked, the more relaxed I began to feel.

There were times I missed aspects of my life in New York, but most of the time the hustle and bustle of city life seemed like nothing more than a distant memory. I considered my time in the city to have been happy and worthwhile, but the longer I lived away from the fast pace and high energy, the more I realized my future was here amid the beauty and quiet of the island.

The rain had begun to come down harder, so I called to Kizzy to let her know it was time to go back. The puppy was adorable and looked like she was having so much fun, but she was completely covered with sand. I hoped I could contain her in the kitchen until she dried out. At least that way I'd only have one room to sweep up.

"Looks like our girl had some fun." Garrett chuckled when the sandy dog and I returned to the warmth of the house.

"She didn't seem to mind the rain in the least." I took a mug from the rack and poured myself a cup of coffee. "I'm going to detain her in here until she dries off and I can brush the sand from her coat."

"Seems like she'll be fine with that idea," George said as Kizzy settled down on her bed in front of the fire.

"Is anyone hungry?" I asked. "I can make us some eggs, and I think we still have sausage from the other day."

The others were hungry, so I began to assemble a meal.

"What time are you and Brit heading over to Abby's?" Clara asked as I fried the sausage links.

"We didn't discuss it. I'm guessing midmorning if Abby is available." I cracked several eggs into a bowl for scrambling. "I really want to help her, but I'm afraid reopening old wounds as we go over the details again and again has to be hard on her. Given her advanced pregnancy, that worries me."

"I don't suppose all the stress she's dealing with can be good for the baby," Garrett agreed.

"I'm hoping we'll catch a break in the next day or two so we can wrap this up sooner rather than later." I set the sausage onto a plate covered with a paper towel before pouring the eggs into the pan I'd prepared.

Clara got up and gathered the plates and utensils we'd need. George refreshed everyone's coffee. When I lived in the city, I almost never ate breakfast, preferring to grab coffee on my way into the office. Having a family to share a meal with most mornings was nice.

"I'll be interested to hear what Rick has to say about Bobby's work schedule and how it compares to the fires," George said. "It seems unlikely he would be able to sneak away to set the fires if he'd been on shift with two other firefighters."

I scooped the scrambled eggs into a bowl and set it on the table. Then I transferred the sausage to a clean plate and set it on the table as well. "Does anyone need anything else?"

"Do you think we should call Vikki to see if she wants to join us?" Clara asked.

"I thought about calling her, but she looked so tired last night. If she's sleeping in, I think we should let her. If she doesn't pop in at some point this morning, I'll go over to her place to check on her."

"Speaking of checking on people, has anyone spoken to Nicole lately?" George asked.

"I chatted with her briefly maybe two weeks ago," I said. "She was on her way out as I passed her cabin while taking a walk. I invited her to join us for another of our group meals because she seemed to enjoy the time she spent with us over Christmas, but she said she had a lot of work to do. Why do you ask?"

"I noticed the light in her cabin has been on for the past three days. It doesn't look like it's been turned off at all, although I haven't been awake in the middle of the night to notice."

I hadn't seen the light, but I'd been busy and not really paying attention. Garrett hadn't been out much with the weather we'd been having, and Clara had seemed content to stay inside as well. George's cabin was closest to Nicole's, so it made sense that he would be the one to notice the light.

"Maybe I should check on her too," I said. "She'll be irritated that I bothered her if everything is fine, but if it isn't, maybe she needs some help."

"That might be a good idea," George said. "I realize she's made it clear she doesn't welcome company, but it does seem odd that she'd leave her light on for such an extended period of time."

George and Clara offered to clean up after breakfast so I could check on Nicole. I considered bringing Kizzy, who she seemed to love, with me, but she'd only just dried off.

As George had said, the overhead light in Nicole's living area was on. I knocked on the door and waited, but there was no answer. I knocked again, but when there was still no response, I used my master key to open the door.

"Nicole," I called, waiting at the threshold for a reply. "It's Jill," I added, taking a step inside. The cabin appeared to be empty, but I took a minute to check all the rooms just in case. The cabin was clean and appeared undisturbed. Perhaps Nicole had left town for a few days and had forgotten to turn off the light.

I turned it off now, and relocked the cabin. I thought about checking on Vikki while I was out but didn't want to wake her if she was sleeping in, and returned to the main house.

"Is everything okay?" George asked.

"Nicole isn't home. I'm wondering if she didn't go out of town for a few days and just forgot to turn off the light."

"Her car is in the drive," George pointed out.

"She might have left with a friend or called for a taxi if she was going to the airport. I have her cell number. I'll give her a call just to be sure."

Nicole didn't answer, so I left a message, asking her to call me, then went upstairs to change. I found that our current investigation was making me anxious. Combined with my worry about Jack, I felt like a walking time bomb about to explode.

******

Brit had called Abby to explain that we wanted to come by to speak with her, so she was waiting when we arrived. The house she was trying desperately to save was clean and well maintained, although the furniture looked to be secondhand and decorative items such as knickknacks and artwork were noticeably missing. Abby invited us to sit down on the sofa before taking a seat herself in a chair across from us.

"Do you have news?" she asked, a tone of anxiety in her voice.

"We just have a few questions for you. I hope that's okay."

Abby nodded. "The twins are napping, so I'll need to keep an ear out for them, but I can talk until they wake up. What did you want to know?"

I leaned forward and attempted to make eye contact with the obviously nervous young woman. "I know talking about this is probably very hard for you and I wouldn't keep asking so many questions if we didn't really need to."

Abby looked at me with huge, sad eyes. "I know. It's okay. Ask me anything you need to."

"According to information I've been given, you'd been out shopping on the day you found Bobby in the garage."

"That's correct. My friend Laurie had taken the kids to the park so I could get some errands done.

Bobby had been on a shift at the firehouse, but he was due to get off at five, so my plan had been to put the groceries away, pick up the kids, and then make dinner."

"So your car must have been parked in the drive?" I asked.

Abby nodded. "I knew I was going to be going out again, so I didn't bother with putting it into the garage."

"Okay, so you parked in the drive and brought in your groceries. Then what happened?"

A tear ran down her cheek as she softly answered. "I smelled exhaust. It didn't occur to me it was car exhaust at first, but I wanted to be sure we didn't have a gas leak or something before I brought the kids home, so I started to look around. I went into the garage and saw Bobby's car. At first, I thought he must have gotten off early for some reason, but then I realized he was sitting in the driver's seat but not making any attempt to get out. I walked over to the car. I realized right away that something was wrong. His seat belt was still buckled. I opened the car door, and it was obvious he was dead. I ran back into the house and called 911."

"So Bobby had been on shift for a regular forty-eight hours and had taken his car with him when he left home," I clarified.

"Yes. That's right."

For some reason, I'd assumed right up to this point that Bobby had been at home and the car had already been in the garage prior to whatever happened that led to his death, but if he had been at work, that meant he must have left early for some reason. Could someone have followed him?

"The report said the car engine had been turned off by the time you found Bobby."

"Yes."

"You're sure you didn't turn it off after finding Bobby was dead?"

Abby shook her head. "It was already off. When I realized he was dead, I ran back to the house and called 911. I didn't go inside the car or do anything else. I was shaking so badly, I couldn't have turned off the ignition even if it had been on. Do you have any idea how shocking it is to find the man you plan to grow old with sitting so naturally even though you know he's dead?"

"Honestly, I can't imagine. It must have been horrible."

"Horrible is putting it mildly. At first there's this flash of disbelief. It's like you know what you're seeing is real, but your mind refuses to accept it. And then comes panic, followed by a deep and intense grief. The minutes right after I found Bobby are still sort of a blur, but if there's one thing I'm certain of, it's that the engine was already turned off when I arrived home."

I glanced at Brit. She offered a look of encouragement but didn't respond. I took a deep breath and then asked my next question. "You mentioned Bobby still had his seat belt on."

"Yes, that's right. I thought maybe he drove home, pulled into the garage, and was met by whoever killed him. I have to believe he was knocked out in some way or he would have tried to get free, but the man who talked to me after Bobby died didn't think anyone else had been here." Abby looked me in the eye. "But someone had to have been here. Right?

Someone knocked Bobby out, put that note in the car, and then closed the garage door. They must have waited until Bobby was dead and then turned off the engine and left. It's the only way it could have happened."

Brit was frowning, but I didn't want to break contact with Abby to see what was on her mind, so I asked my next question. "You said Bobby was at work and wasn't due home until five. He obviously left the firehouse early. Has anyone ever said why?"

Abby paused. Her eyes flickered, as if she was trying to remember. "No. I don't think the reason for Bobby being home early ever came up."

I made a mental note to check it out. "After you called 911, who showed up first?"

"Captain Oliver. He got here real quick. He told me to wait in the house and he would take care of everything."

"Captain Oliver is the fire chief where Bobby was assigned?" I clarified.

"Yes, ma'am. He said he was heading back to the firehouse after responding to a medical emergency in the neighborhood, so he was close by when the call came over the radio. He came straight over. I'm not sure what happened after that. I waited inside until one of the deputies came in and began asking me questions. I was in shock at that point. I barely remember even answering."

"I understand you had just found out your husband was dead and things must have seemed almost surreal, but is there anything you can remember from that day that struck you as odd? Anything that stood out as not being quite right?"

Abby glanced toward the window and then back at me. She frowned but didn't answer right away. Then she began to speak. "There is one thing that seemed odd. It's probably nothing, but after everyone left, I noticed the mailbox out by the street was leaning to the side and had a dent in it. It looked like maybe someone had run into it. I figured maybe one of the vehicles that responded to the 911 call had backed into it, but the paint that had been left on the mailbox was green. None of the emergency vehicles were green."

"And you're sure the mailbox was undamaged when you left to go shopping?" I asked.

"Pretty sure. The mail hadn't come for the day yet when I left, so there was no reason for me to check it, but it was leaning quite a bit afterward, so it would seem I would have noticed."

"Do you remember noticing if it was leaning when you came home with the groceries?"

Abby shook her head. "No. I don't remember noticing one way or the other."

It occurred to me that it might be worthwhile to speak with the neighbors. If someone had noticed a car at the house earlier in the day—a green one, to be specific—it was possible someone might have seen a killer.

After we left Abby's, Brit and I decided to go over to Rick's office. Not only was I curious about whether it had been possible to track down Bobby's whereabouts during the five fires, but I wanted to speak to him about our conversation with Abby.

"I was just about to call you," Rick said when Brit and I entered the reception area.

"Did you find something?"

"According to interviews conducted at the time of Bobby's death, he was at the firehouse during the first, second, and fourth fire, and at home during the third and fifth."

"So Bobby couldn't have set the first, second, and fourth fires," Brit said.

"Definitely not the first one. The fire was called in at ten-fifteen, so the rest of the crew would most likely still have been awake and would have noticed if he left. The second fire was called in at two-thirty a.m., the fourth at three-ten a.m., so it's possible, although highly improbable, that Bobby could have snuck out while the others slept, started the fire, and then snuck back in before it was reported."

"It would be some feat to pull that off," I said.

"I agree. It does look as if he's at least innocent of setting the first, second, and fourth fire. It seems unlikely he was able to sneak out to set the third and fifth fires, which occurred when he was at home, without anyone noticing but not impossible. Especially if Abby is a sound sleeper."

"Even if he snuck out while Abby slept and started the third and fifth fires, why would he leave a suicide note accepting responsibility for all five?"

"He didn't actually claim responsibility for all five," Rick answered. "I took another look at the note he supposedly wrote. It says he's *responsible for a man's death* and that's *something he can't live with.* It's possible he's only responsible for setting the fifth and only deadly fire."

I leaned against the counter. "That makes no sense. If there was a serial arsonist out there, why would Bobby suddenly decide to set a fire of his own?"

Rick shrugged. "I don't know. I'm not saying he did. As we've said from the beginning, it's possible the suicide note was a fake."

I hated that this case seemed to be getting more and more confusing with each new piece of information we uncovered. "Brit and I spoke to Abby this morning," I said, deciding to move on to the news we had to share. "We discovered two interesting facts. One was that Bobby had been on shift on the day he was found dead. He hadn't been scheduled to get off until five, but Abby discovered his body in the garage earlier in the afternoon. She didn't specify a time, but I got the impression it was an hour or two before he was due home. I asked her if she knew why he had come home early and she said she didn't."

Rick's gaze narrowed. "I wonder if anyone ever checked that out."

"I don't know. I was hoping you did."

"I'll look in to it and let you know what I find. Anything else?"

"Abby said that after all the emergency vehicles left, she noticed her mailbox was tilted to one side. She figured one of the vehicles might have backed into it, but she noticed a dent in the box with green paint around it. She pointed out that none of the emergency vehicles were green."

"Maybe the mailbox was already dented."

"She said she didn't think so," I told Rick. "I thought it might be worth our while to talk to the neighbors to see if any of them noticed a green car in the Bostons' drive on the day Bobby died."

"I agree. It's been six months, so we may have a hard time finding anyone who can remember that far back, but it wouldn't hurt to put out some feelers. Anything else?"

I glanced at Brit. She shook her head. "I guess that's it for now. Brit and I were going to try to speak to the property owners from the five fires to see if anything pops. If you find out anything important, call me."

"You might want to tread lightly when speaking to the fire victims. I know you can dig in and go for the kill when you're working an angle for a story, but remember, these people have already been through a lot."

"Don't worry. I'll play nice."

By the time Brit and I left Rick's office it was time for lunch. The deli was just down the street, but at Gertie's you could usually pick up a side of gossip to go along with your sandwich. I couldn't help but glance at my phone as I plugged it into the car charger. Still no message from Jack. What on earth could be going on that he couldn't take a minute to answer my text?

"Everything okay?" Brit asked as I pulled onto the highway and headed toward the wharf.

"Everything's fine. I was just wondering how Jack's doing."

"He still hasn't called?"

I shook my head.

"He will," Brit assured me. "Parent and child relationships can be complicated."

"Tell me about it. I haven't seen my own mother in years, and when we do speak, it's short and to the point. I know Jack is closer to his mother than I am to mine, though, and I really hoped I'd have a chance to meet her."

"It's best to let Jack control the timing of the introduction of his mother to his girlfriend. I wonder what she's like."

"She sounds like a tyrant. I keep picturing this huge, overpowering woman ruling over poor Jack with an iron fist."

Brit picked up her phone and punched in a few commands. "Based on this photo, it appears she's petite, with long dark hair and the skin of a twenty-year-old."

"Must be touched up," I countered.

Brit shrugged. "Maybe. But if I were you, I'd go into this with the mind-set that you're going to like Jack's mother. Nothing good can come from you deciding you hate her before you even meet her."

"I guess you have a point," I acknowledged. "The thing is, I don't even know what the problem is between Jack and his mother. I just keep picturing her bullying him into moving back to New York, which would effectively tear him from my life."

"Jack cares about you. He would never let that happen."

I hoped Brit was right.

Chapter 7

Gertie's was packed, as it usually was at that time of day. There was one booth free in the cove overlooking the marina, but it had a "Reserved" sign on it, so Brit and I took seats at the counter. We both ordered soup and individual loaves of hot bread. The rain that had been coming and going all day was back, so it was a dreary view out the windows overlooking the harbor.

"How did your chat with Abby go?" Gertie asked after setting our food in front of us.

"It went fine." I took a small bite of the thick, creamy lobster chowder. "I could see it was hard for her to talk about finding Bobby dead in the garage, but she did a good job of maintaining her composure. Things went down differently from what I initially imagined."

"Oh, and how's that?"

I reluctantly set down my spoon before answering the question. In my opinion, I made a pretty good soup, but Gertie certainly had a magical touch. "For one thing, Bobby had been at work on the day he died. He wasn't due home until five, yet Abby found his body in the garage before that. I can't help but wonder why he left early. And I wonder why that never came up in the initial investigation. You would think someone would have mentioned it at some point along the way. Of course, maybe it was mentioned, and we just haven't come across it."

"It seems you're tryin' to cover a lot of territory in a short amount of time. It's not surprisin' things might be overlooked."

I picked up my spoon and took another bite of food. "You usually have a good take on things. What do you think we might be missing?"

"I'm not rightly sure, but Quinten and I spoke after we left your place last night, and he told me it feels like something is missin' from the autopsy report."

"Something like what?"

"He either didn't know or didn't want to say until he had a chance to look at things again. I suppose it's possible there could have been clues at the scene or details about the death that someone tried to cover up. Bobby was a firefighter, and it was his fellow firefighters who showed up first to the 911 call. Maybe they found something they knew would be incriminatin', so they made it disappear before law enforcement arrived."

"What could be more incriminating than a suicide note basically confessing to killing a man?"

Gertie shrugged. "I'm not sayin' I know anythin', I'm just sayin' I have a feelin' there's more goin' on than meets the eye."

I certainly hoped Gertie was wrong because as far as my eye was concerned, there was already too much going on to make sense of things. I returned my attention to my soup and Gertie left to serve other customers. I'd found all the cases the Mastermind Group had taken on interesting, but this was the first one I felt desperate about solving. A woman's ability to care for her children appeared to depend on whether we could prove something that might not be provable.

"Don't turn around, but Jack just walked in the front door," Brit whispered from beside me.

Of course I couldn't help but turn around. Standing next to Jack at the hostess station was the most beautiful woman I'd ever seen. I put my hand over my mouth to make certain it wasn't hanging open as I watched the pair talking and smiling as if they were the best of friends.

"Is that his mother?" I whispered after turning back to Brit.

"I think so. And they're coming this way."

Of course they were. I'd imagined meeting Jack's mother many times, and in each of those daydreams, I'd been looking professional and pulled together, not like a drowned rat with frizzy hair who'd been running around in the rain all day.

"Jack, how nice to see you," I said in a cheery voice that was only slightly more fake than the nonsensical words coming out of my mouth, considering I'd slept with him two nights earlier. Or at least I'd slept with casual, easygoing Jack Jones. The man in front of me had not only put on a suit and tie but he'd blown dry and styled his hair. In many ways, he didn't look a thing like the Jack I had fallen in love with.

Jack smiled back at me, but the look in his eyes was guarded. Apparently, he was no more thrilled to see me than I was to see him. "Mother, I'd like you to meet Jillian Hanford. Jillian, this is my mother, Raquel Jones."

I found myself wishing for a wormhole through which to escape as I offered the woman a smile and a handshake. She ignored the hand but returned the smile.

"You must be Jackson's journalist friend from New York."

Journalist friend? I was hoping for girlfriend, but okay. I nodded and tried to think of something clever to say, but my mind had gone completely blank, so I blurted out the first thing that came to mind. "Yes, I'm a journalist, and while I used to live in New York, I live on Gull Island now, and work at the newspaper with Jack."

"I see." She looked me up and down. "And why is that?"

I hesitated. "Excuse me?"

"Why did you leave a promising career in New York to work on a small weekly paper in the swamplands of South Carolina?"

I glanced at Jack, unsure how to answer. Jack glanced back at me with a look of apology in his eyes.

"It looks like Denton is here," Jack said, glancing toward the door, where another man in a suit stood. "We should find our table." Jack took his mother by the elbow. "It was good seeing you, Jill."

I watched in stunned silence as he led his mother to the table that had been reserved in the little nook that overlooked the marina. The men shook hands, and then Jack, his mother, and the man all took their seats.

"Oh my God," Brit whispered. "What on earth was that all about?"

"I wish I knew."

"Do you want to go?"

I nodded. I tossed a twenty-dollar bill on the counter before getting to my feet and walking as quickly as I could out of the restaurant and, more probably, out of Jack's life.

"Don't read anything into whatever that was," Brit said the minute we got into the car.

"How can I not read anything into it? The man I've been sleeping with for the past several months just treated me like a casual acquaintance he happened to run into."

"I know," Brit said. "I was there. But you don't have the whole story."

"What story?" I screeched. "Jack is obviously ashamed of me. I suppose if you really think about it, I don't live up to the standards of someone who would be seen in public with the great Jackson Jones."

Brit buckled her seat belt, then adjusted it for fit. "Don't be silly. Jack has been seen with you in public lots of times."

"Jack. Not Jackson. I think I may have just met Jackson for the first time."

Brit didn't argue with that point, I imagined because she knew it was true. I'd known Jack had two lives, but what I hadn't realized was that Jack Jones, the easygoing newspaper owner, and Jackson Jones, the world-famous author, were about as much alike as peanut butter and caviar.

I grabbed my phone and took a minute to look at my emails before starting the car. I needed to calm down and get my rage under control. The last thing I wanted to do was take my anger out on the car's accelerator with the roads still damp from the on-and-off rain we'd been having.

"Hannah Smith was the fourth victim of the arsonist, right?" I asked Brit.

"Yes," Brit confirmed. "Hannah was the artist who lost her detached garage as well as her artwork. Why do you ask?"

"I have an email from a Hannah Smith asking if the newspaper would publish a feature about the new art studio she's opening in town."

"I guess we know what she did with her insurance payout. When does she want to meet?"

I turned and glanced at Brit. "At my earliest convenience. Maybe we should go talk to her right now. I need a couple of pieces as filler for the next edition, and we might be able to get a look at the arsons in the area from another perspective."

"I'm in."

"She left a number." I quickly texted the woman and asked if she was available now. I only had to wait thirty seconds for her to say she'd love to see me. She provided the address, which I repeated to Brit. I'd leaned forward and reached out to slip the key in the ignition when my phone pinged again. I looked at the text and frowned.

"Did she change her mind?" Brit asked.

"It's not Hannah, it's Jack."

I turned the phone so Brit could see the text, which read, *I'm sorry. I'll explain later.*

"I guess that's something," Brit offered.

Maybe the text was something, but in my mind, I wasn't sure it was enough.

******

Hannah's gallery was in a visible location, in the middle of the touristy part of town, which got a lot of foot traffic, especially during the summer, so I wouldn't be at all surprised if her venture turned out to be a huge success.

"Thank you so much for getting back to me so soon," Hannah greeted me as Brit and I entered through the stained-glass doorway. My first thought was that a glass door didn't provide much security for an art studio, but then I noticed a second door that was made from sturdy aluminum.

"You caught me at a good time. I was just thinking I needed an additional article or two for the next issue of the paper."

"Oh, I do love it when serendipity is at work." The young woman with a headful of curly hair beamed. "Can I get you a something to drink?"

"Thank you, but we just had lunch," I answered. "Why don't you show us around and we can talk after the tour."

When I'd first heard the story of the woman with a studio in her garage who had lost all her art in a fire just weeks before her first big showing, I imagined an amateur artist who was just as happy to have the insurance money. But as Hannah showed us around her new enterprise, I could feel the love she had for each and every one of her pieces. She referred to them as the children of her soul. The longer Hannah spoke, the clearer it became that the fire that had taken Hannah's work hadn't been a victimless crime at all, despite the insurance payout.

"Your pieces are really wonderful," Brit gushed as we completed our tour. "The emotion you put into each one really comes through. As an observer, I can almost feel what you did when you painted them."

Hannah grinned. "It means a lot to hear you say that."

"When you emailed, I thought your name sounded familiar, so I looked you up and realized you were the artist who lost a lot of your work in a fire."

Hannah nodded. "The fire was something of a double-edged sword. The insurance money allowed me to open this place, but I don't think people understand how hard it was to lose my work. Even the fire chief commented that at least I was fully insured, so I didn't really lose anything. Seriously? The art I lost had meaning to me. It wasn't simply a means to a paycheck."

"I get it," Brit said. "Most people don't understand that artists put part of their souls into everything they create."

Hannah indicated that we should have a seat at a long table she had set against a wall. I figured this would be as good a place as any for the interview and was anxious to get started.

"I want to speak with you about your plans for the studio, but because the fire has come up, I'd like to ask a few questions about that as well for another article I'm writing."

"Okay. I guess that would be all right."

"I understand you were the fourth victim of the arsonist?"

"Yes. My studio burned after the bakery and before the house that took a man's life. I guess I was lucky I was away and that no harm came to either myself or my house. It could have been worse."

"Have you ever stopped to ask yourself why you were targeted?" I asked.

"What do you mean?"

"Of all the structures on the island, why your studio?"

Hannah frowned. "I don't know. I guess I never stopped to think about it."

"Do you know the other victims?"

Hannah shook her head. "No. I've never met any of them. I only moved to the island a couple of years ago and I keep to myself most of the time."

"Where exactly were you when the fire occurred?" I wondered.

"In New York. After I heard the gallery wanted to feature some of my work in their next showing, I decided to visit it to familiarize myself with the layout. I was only going to be gone for a week. The fire occurred on the second day I was away."

I pulled a notepad out of my bag, flipped it open, and clicked open my pen. "Who knew that you weren't going to be here?"

"I called the gallery in New York and told them I would be coming by, and of course I reserved a flight and hotel room. My sister, who lives in California, knew where I was going and the dates I would be there, but other than that, I didn't tell anyone. Except for the cleaning service, of course."

"Cleaning service?"

"I'm not much of a housekeeper, so I have a service that comes in once a week to do the floors and the dusting. I knew I wouldn't be home on their regular day, and I prefer to be here when they're working, so I let them know I was skipping that week."

"Would you be willing to provide me with the name and number of the service you use?"

"Sure." Hannah stood up. "I'll grab the information for you."

Once I had that information, I moved on to things about the studio that I'd need for the article. I could write it up tonight and submit it in time for next week's issue. After the interview, Brit and I returned to my car.

"Her place is really great," Brit said after we were settled.

"It was very nice. A lot nicer than I was expecting. I guess I was somehow thinking she was more of a dabbler."

"We knew she'd been given space in a New York gallery," Brit pointed out.

"True. I suppose I just let that fact pass over me." I slipped my key in the ignition, then paused. "What do you think about the cleaning service?"

"I think she's smart to outsource her housework if she doesn't enjoy it."

"What I mean is, what do you think about it as a link between the victims?"

Brit turned in her seat. "I'm not following."

"All of the victims were off the island when the arsonist struck. My question is, how did the arsonist find out who would be gone when?"

"You think they all used the same cleaning service?"

I shrugged. "It isn't outside the realm of possibility. Besides, it would be easy to check out. How about we see if we can't score an interview with a few of the other fire victims?"

Brit pulled out her iPad and did some digging. She found Pop still lived on the island, and still fished for a living. We thought he'd most likely be found at the marina later in the afternoon. Jasper Wells, whose barn had burned, worked at a feed and tackle store on the next island over, and Hillary Tisdale, the bakeshop owner, had left the island to rebuild elsewhere. The only victim we couldn't find information on was the man whose friend had died when his house burned down. We decided to try to speak to Pop and Wells. If they used the same cleaning service as Hannah, we'd fill Rick in and let him track down the last two victims.

"Let's start with Jasper Wells," I said. "Maybe by the time we get back to Gull Island, Pop will have returned to the marina for the day."

"It's about a thirty-minute drive," Brit informed me.

"I have a couple of articles to write, but I can do that this evening. Do you have time to come along?"

"I don't have any plans for today. Let's go chat with Wells and take things from there."

As it turned out, Jasper Wells confirmed that his wife did use a weekly cleaning service. He called to ask her the name, which turned out to be the same one Hannah used. We headed to the marina to talk with Pop, who was guarded in his answers, a whole lot less forthcoming than the other two victims we'd spoken to, but when we asked about a cleaning service, he snorted and asked where in the hell he would get money for a hoity-toity thing like that.

"What now?" Brit asked. "We have two victims who used the cleaning service, one who didn't, and two whose current whereabouts are unknown."

"Let's head back to the resort. I left Kizzy with George, who might want a break from the energetic little darling by now. Then I'll make a few calls. Even though only two of the five victims have confirmed they used the cleaning service, I think that's enough to bring it to Rick's attention."

When we arrived at the resort we found Garrett, George, and Clara playing cards. Kizzy had been sleeping by the fire, but the minute she saw me, she came running over to say hi. "How's my Kizzy Q?" I asked as I vigorously scratched the puppy's neck. "Did you miss me?"

Based on the amount of jumping around the puppy was doing, it looked like she had.

"How'd it go?" George asked.

"Brit can fill you in while I take Kizzy out. I won't be gone long. When I get back, we can talk further."

The minute I opened the back door, Kizzy ran out into the damp yard. She was bouncing around like a bronco at the rodeo, which indicated to me she had excess energy to burn. I started toward the beach and she happily followed. The air was still damp, but the rain had stopped, at least temporarily.

I took a deep breath and willed myself to relax. It had been a stressful day, but I was walking on a beach with a puppy I simply adored. No matter what was going on with Jack and his barracuda of a mother, life certainly could be worse.

I pulled my phone out of my pocket and looked at his text again. He said he was sorry and would explain later. I wondered when *later* would be. Later today? After his mom left the island? After he packed up his things and returned to his life as Jackson Jones?

The situation was giving me indigestion, so I willed myself to think of something else. Anything else.

I knew that on some level, Jack cared about me and would never intentionally hurt me, but on another—the level that seemed to be much closer to the surface—I was hurt and angry that if forced to make a choice between me and his mother, he hadn't chosen me. I knew mother-and-son relationships could be complicated, but somehow, I'd thought the bond between the two of us meant just as much.

Of course, I may have been fooling myself. Jack and I hadn't even known each other for a year, and we'd only been romantically involved for the past three months. Had it only been three months? It seemed longer. I guess if I looked at things objectively, I could see why Jack might not want to drive a wedge between himself and his mother over a woman he'd known for six months, been dating for three months, and had only slept with a couple of dozen times.

I called to Kizzy, who had wandered down the beach farther than I was comfortable with. She immediately ran back toward me. We hadn't been walking all that long, but I was becoming more and more agitated, so I decided to turn back to the house.

As I passed the cabins, I noticed Vikki's was empty. I'd called her earlier to check in because she'd never come by, and she'd mentioned meeting a friend in Charleston today. Alex's cabin was empty as well, but he came and went, rarely bothering to inform anyone of his plans.

When I arrived at Nicole's cabin, I saw the interior was dark. It had been each time I'd looked in this direction since I'd turned off the light the previous day. I walked slowly to the front door and knocked.

"Nicole," I called out. "It's Jill and Kizzy."

No answer.

I tried again, but the result was the same. I didn't have my master key with me, so I continued to the main house. I knew Nicole was an adult who had never had any sort of inclination to keep the rest of us apprised of her whereabouts, but for some reason, I was getting worried. It could be the fact that she hadn't taken her car with her, and she hadn't answered her phone or returned any of my messages. Of course, knowing Nicole, she could simply be ignoring me. It certainly wouldn't be the first time. Still, I hoped she would return soon so the nagging little voice in the back of my mind would be quiet.

Chapter 8

When I returned to the house, the others were discussing whether the cleaning service or one of its employees could be linked to the arsons. Brit had taken the initiative in calling Rick, who had promised to look in to the idea. If an employee of the cleaning service was either the arsonist or was connected to the arsonist, and all the fire victims were clients, it could explain how they knew who was out of town and when. Still, Pop clearly hadn't been a customer. I supposed the arsonist could have known he'd be out of town by some other means, and perhaps they only started connecting with cleaning-service clients after the first fire.

I wasn't sure how identifying the arsonist would prove Bobby had been murdered unless it was the arsonist who'd killed him, and we could make the connection. If that was the case, trying to identify the arsonist made sense.

Once I had dried at least some of the moisture from Kizzy's coat, I poured myself a cup of hot coffee and joined the others at the table. The fire in the kitchen fireplace had been maintained throughout the day, so the room was nice and warm. If it wasn't for the situation with Jack hanging over my head, I would probably enjoy an afternoon brainstorming session with my friends.

"Before I forget, did you hear from Vikki?" asked George.

"I spoke to her just before lunch. She's in Charleston today."

"And Nicole?"

"I still haven't heard from her."

"She's probably off doing research or something," Brit said. "It's not like she ever checks in with us. In fact, if anything, her pattern is to push us away as much as possible."

"Brit's right," I said. "I'm sure Nicole is fine. I'm going to grab a plate of cookies to go with this coffee. Does anyone want anything else?"

I'd just returned to the table with plenty of cookies to share when I saw I had a call. "I'm going to take this in the other room," I said.

I went into the living room before I clicked the Answer button.

"Good afternoon, Mr. Jones," I said with an icy tone.

"I guess I deserve that. I'm sorry about Gertie's."

"In this case, I'm not sure *I'm sorry* is going to cut it."

Jack let out a long breath. "I know. The situation caught me off guard and I handled it badly."

I wanted to believe he really was sorry, but I guess I wasn't over being mad because rather than accepting his apology, I kept quiet.

"I'm afraid I made one mistake after the other today," Jack continued. "I should have realized when my mom's friend Denton suggested Gertie's for lunch there was a better-than-average chance of running into you there. If I had insisted on meeting elsewhere, the whole thing could have been avoided."

"So, you *are* trying to avoid me," I said in a voice that was so high it didn't sound like my own.

"Yes. I mean, no. I'm just making this worse, aren't I?"

"A little bit."

I listened as Jack let out a sigh. I could picture him running his hand through his hair. I waited silently for him to make up his mind where this conversation was heading. Finally, he spoke. "I can't think of a single way to explain what's going on without sounding like a sniveling mama's boy without a will of his own."

"It already looks that way, so I don't think you can make things worse," I snapped back. Even I flinched when I realized how harsh that sounded.

I considered taking it back, but then Jack began to speak. "You have to understand. My mother is very important to me. She raised me on her own, giving up so much of her own life to make sure I had as many advantages as she could provide. She worked two jobs when I was young and three so I could go to college. That should have been enough. I was on track to graduate college and go into journalism, and then she'd finally have time to pursue her own dreams. But then I wrote that first best seller and again she put her life on hold to help me build my career. And she did a wonderful job. There's no doubt in my mind that it was her hard work that allowed me to end up where I have. My mother has always been there for me. More so than anyone else in my life."

Okay, that stung more than I would have liked.

"I guess I have a hard time saying no to her." Jack took another deep breath before he continued. "Having said that, I also realize she has a way of thinking she knows what's best for me whether I have a differing viewpoint or not. For most of my life, I've gone along with her to avoid a conflict. I think the first really big fight we had was when I told her I was buying the paper and moving to the island. She accused me of throwing away the career she'd given up everything to help me build, but I was adamant and insisted I needed some time to step out of the limelight and unwind. She finally gave in and agreed to take a step back so I could take the time I needed."

"It is your life," I pointed out.

"I know. I think she knows it to, and that scares her. When my dad left, I became the center of her world and now that I'm gone…"

"Okay, I get it. But what does that mean? Are you going back to New York?" I asked.

"No. I am absolutely not going back to New York, but I'm trying to find a way to make my mother understand that I've thought this through and am making my decision based on what I and I alone believe is best for me. When I told her I wanted to turn down the book deal and the money that comes with it, she accused me of letting some woman get into my head and manipulate me into making a decision that wasn't in my best interest. I assured her that no one was manipulating me, but I could see she didn't believe me. If I introduce you as my girlfriend now, she'll be more convinced than ever that you're Satan and have led me astray. But if I agree to meet with the publisher and at least discuss the deal, and then decide after everything is on the table that the series isn't the direction I want to go in my career, she can't accuse me of not making my own decision based on the facts I've been given."

"And if she still doesn't accept your decision?" I had to ask.

"Then she doesn't. I promise you, I'm not moving back to New York, and I promise you, our relationship and the future we're beginning to build are the most important thing to me, but I want to at least try to set a pace that will leave room for my mom and you to have a relationship in the future. I know she'll come around when she sees my mind really is made up, and I know she'll love you if she's able to meet you at a time when she doesn't consider you a threat."

I wasn't sure how I felt about all this, but I knew I didn't want to do anything to sever my relationship with Jack. "Okay," I eventually said. "I can give you the space you need. Call me after she leaves."

"I will. And again, I'm sorry. I'll make it up to you."

I said something noncommittal and hung up.

I understood what Jack was saying, but I wasn't sure his mother and any woman he ever became serious about would be able to have a relationship. If you asked me, she seemed to be the sort of person who would never be willing to share.

By the time I returned to the kitchen, Rick had called Brit back and the others had a new topic to discuss. Apparently, the bakery shop owner had used the same cleaning service as the barn and art studio owner, which meant there was a good probability the company or one of its employees was in some way involved in the arsons.

******

Although I'd made the decision to head up to bed early that night, sleep was eluding me. It wasn't all that late, so I pulled on some warm clothes and went downstairs with Kizzy on my heels. I was still feeling angsty and agitated. Perhaps a brisk walk followed by some warm milk would be what I needed to calm my mind enough to allow sleep to take over. As I often do, I was going to head to the beach, but at the last minute I took a detour and took the walkway that connected the cabins. I was sure Vikki must be back, but she hadn't stopped by the house, so I headed in her direction on the chance she was still awake. When I saw her light was on, I walked up to the front door and knocked.

"Jill?" Vikki greeted. "Is everything okay?"

"Everything is fine. I couldn't sleep, so Kizzy and I went for a walk. I saw your light on, but if this isn't a good time…"

Vikki opened the door wider. "No. It's fine. Come on in. Can I get you anything? Wine?"

"I'm fine, thanks. When I realized you were up, I figured I'd stop by to see how your lunch in Charleston went."

Vikki looked confused for a moment, but she quickly recovered. "It was fine. How were things here?"

I paused before answering. "Are you okay? It seems like maybe you haven't been feeling well lately."

"I'm fine."

I frowned as I noticed a tear in the corner of her eye. I took her hand in mine. "You know you can talk to me about anything."

Vikki dipped her head. She didn't speak, but the tear slipped down her cheek.

"Come on, Vik. Talk to me. Maybe I can help."

Vikki looked up and wiped the tear from her cheek with the back of her hand. "I wasn't having lunch with a friend today. I was in Charleston seeing a doctor for a second opinion."

"A doctor? Are you sick?"

"I'm not sick. I have uterine cysts. I've had them for years, but they're getting worse. My doctor feels we should remove them, and given the fact that my mother died of uterine cancer, he's recommending a complete hysterectomy."

My face softened. "Oh, hon. I'm so sorry."

Vikki looked me in the eye. "You know, if this had come up a year ago, I would have had the surgery and never given it a second thought. I lived a very active life and my relationships with men were always short-lived. Getting married and becoming a mother someday were nowhere on my radar."

"And then you met Rick."

Vikki stood up and began to pace. "And then I met Rick."

"Have you talked about marriage and kids?"

Vikki shook her head. "No. It's much too early for that, but it's something that feels like an actual possibility for the first time in my life. Rick has mentioned that he wants to get married and have a family someday, and he's told me on more than one occasion how important our relationship is to him. I guess I would be lying if I didn't admit I've envisioned us growing old together."

"Have you told him? About the surgery?"

"No. And I'm not going to. Doing so would present something we aren't ready to deal with. I've pretty much decided to get all the facts and then make a decision on my own based on my options."

"Are you sure?"

"Yes. It isn't fair to him to make him part of the equation. It would add a level of commitment and responsibility to a relationship that's still new."

I sat back, trying to understand what Vikki was saying. It did seem she'd thought things through. "What exactly do you mean by commitment and responsibility?"

"Suppose I decided not to have the hysterectomy for no other reason than to maybe someday provide Rick with the children I know he wants. What if after not having the hysterectomy, I develop cancer at some point in the future? I can't see how he wouldn't feel responsible in some way. I don't want to put that on him. If we were married or even engaged, it might make sense to make the decision together, but we aren't."

"You aren't going to be able to avoid telling him," I said. "Whichever route you take, he's going to know there's something going on."

"I know. But when I tell him, I want to have already made up my mind." Vikki stopped pacing and sat back down. "I just wish I knew what to do."

"What are the pros and cons?" I asked.

"The big pro of having the hysterectomy is that I eliminate the possibility of getting uterine cancer, which I'm at high risk for, given my background and medical history. The con is that I'll never have children. Part of me wonders if I want to have them anyway. I'm not over the hill but, at thirty-eight, I'm not exactly a spring chicken when it comes to my reproductive age. I have a life and a career I love. A life and a career, by the way, that really don't mesh with motherhood."

"And if you don't have the hysterectomy?"

"I leave the door open to having children, but I risk getting cancer. Six months ago, I couldn't imagine ever wanting to give up what I have to settle down and raise a family, and to be honest, I'm pretty sure I'm not there yet. But there's a tiny crack in the door that at least has opened my mind to the possibility. I guess if I'm totally honest, my biggest hesitation is how this will affect Rick and our relationship. If I have the surgery, do I just break up with him, knowing he wants a family? And if I don't break up with him and we do fall helplessly in love and marry, will he always regret that he wasn't able to have a child of his own, and will I feel guilty for not giving him one?"

"You're facing the same dilemma I did last month, when I was trying to decide whether to accept Margo's job offer. I was trying to make a decision based on a relationship that may not even exist in the future."

"Exactly."

"I understand your desire to leave the relationship out of the picture, but is that even possible?"

Vikki groaned and put her hands over her head. "I don't know."

I supposed Jack might be dealing with the same dilemma in a way. He'd said he told his mother his decision regarding the book deal had nothing to do with me, but did it? If I hadn't been in the picture, might he have been more apt to jump on what sounded like a great opportunity? And if our relationship was part of the equation, did I even want it to be? Our relationship was fairly new, and while I valued it greatly, I wasn't sure I wanted to be responsible for Jack walking away from something that might be good for his career. What if our feelings changed? What if mine did?

Chapter 9

Friday, January 26

I woke on Friday with a new sense of determination. It would be easy to get bogged down in my fear that Jack's mother would somehow talk him into leaving Gull Island or my worry about Vikki and the tough decision she faced, but neither decision was mine to make, and I've found it's best to focus on things over which you had some level of control. I pulled on some sweats and took Kizzy out for a quick run.

The weather had changed. Not only was it sunny, without a trace of a cloud in the sky, but it felt like Mother Nature planned to grant us an unseasonably warm day as well. I had my articles to file for the newspaper this morning and I was meeting Brooke for lunch, but maybe Kizzy and I would take a long hike in the afternoon.

Of course, there was still the issue of Bobby's death to resolve. Although we had uncovered a number of random facts that seemed to be relevant, I still had no idea how they fit together, or even if a complete picture would give us the most important answer we were looking for. I couldn't imagine how hard this must be for Abby. The grief involved in losing your husband so expectedly at such a young age must be almost unimaginable in isolation, but add in five children and a mountain of debt, and I was surprised she was holding it together as well as she seemed to be.

I had just made the turn at the end of the eastern side of the peninsula that led to the turtle beach when I saw Alex dressed in a running suit, talking on the phone. I was surprised to see him up so early. He tended to party late and sleep in past noon, but it appeared he'd had the same idea I had about a morning run. Once Kizzy saw him, she took off in his direction, so I changed direction as well and followed her. By the time I arrived at the place where he was standing, he'd finished his call.

"I see we had the same idea," I said as he bent over to pet Kizzy.

"It's the first totally sunny morning we've had in quite some time. I figured I should take advantage of it while I had the chance."

"Kizzy and I didn't mean to interrupt you."

Alex picked up a stick and threw it for the puppy, who immediately took off after it. "No problem. I'm glad I ran into you. I haven't been around much, but I did follow up with the men I know who work in Bobby's firehouse."

I used a hand to shade the sun from my eyes. "And...?"

"According to the guys, Bobby was a hardworking and well-liked addition to the firehouse. A couple of the guys confirm that his stress level seemed to increase dramatically when he found out Abby was pregnant, but those same men said he seemed to be handling it. I asked about the layoffs and have confirmed that prior to the arson spree, there was talk about reducing the three-man crews to two-man crews during the overnight hours as a means of reducing the budget."

"So the cuts were never made?"

"No. After the arsons, the captain was able to argue that a hot and destructive fire can occur at any time of the day or night and without warning. He argued that it would be careless to try to provide fire protection with less than three men."

"So if Bobby set the fires to save his job, it looks like it worked."

"I guess it did."

Alex started to walk down the beach and I fell into step behind him. "Do you know how many men were looking at layoffs?" I asked, wanting to confirm what I had learned.

"At least two. Bobby and one other man who was hired just before he was."

"Do you know the name of the other man?"

"Sam Petrie. According to the other guys, Bobby and Sam got along okay, but both were ambitious and there seemed to be something of a rivalry between them. I considered the fact that if Bobby had been setting the fires, Sam may have found out and threatened to tell, but that only makes sense if Sam was the firefighter who ended up dead."

I stopped walking. I turned and looked at Alex. "What if Sam was the arsonist and Bobby found out and threatened to tell?"

Alex paused. "I guess that works. He was looking at a layoff, the same as Bobby."

"I asked Rick to compare Bobby's work schedule with the fires; maybe I should have him compare the fires with Sam's schedule."

"It couldn't hurt. And while you're at it, find out if they were off shift at different times. It seems because they were both new, they would be on different teams. Maybe they worked together and alternated setting the fires on their off nights. It would be a smart way to provide both with an alibi for at least some of the fires."

I smiled. "Thanks, Alex. I think you might be on to something."

Kizzy and I returned to the house and I fed her, then headed upstairs to shower and change. The breakfast crew hadn't shown up yet, so perhaps I'd make some muffins to serve once they did. I combed out my wet hair, pulled on some jeans and a sweater, and headed back to the first story of the house. I could hear voices in the distance and the wonderful smell of something baking, so perhaps Clara had risen after I'd gone up to my suite in the attic and started the muffins in my absence.

"It smells like you read my mind again," I said to Clara after entering the kitchen. "Blueberry?"

"Of course, dear. It's what you were craving."

"It's exactly what I was craving." I poured myself a cup of coffee and opened the refrigerator. "I'll make a nice fruit salad to go with it."

"Did you enjoy your run?"

I wasn't going to ask how Clara knew that was what I'd done. "Yes. It's a beautiful morning, which has made me in the mood for spring."

"The hot weather will be here soon enough. I'm enjoying the cooler weather we've been having. Did Alex say whether he'd join us for breakfast?"

"He didn't say, but it seemed he had somewhere to go. I can hear Garrett moving around in his room, and I'm sure George will be by. I think Vikki had a late night, so I hate to call and wake her. If she doesn't come over, I'll take her some muffins later."

"Any sign of Nicole?" Clara began setting plates and utensils on the table.

"I didn't go by her place while I was out, but I think I'll pop by later in the morning. I can't help thinking something's wrong, but if Nicole hadn't left her light on, we may not even have realized she'd been away."

"I don't have a sense she's in danger, so perhaps you're correct. I picked up some fresh honey while I was in town the other day. Perhaps I'll have some with my tea."

"I'll grab it," I said as I opened the pantry door.

"Something smells good," Garrett said as he came into the room with Blackbeard on his shoulder.

"Kill the cat, kill the cat," Blackbeard said after taking one look at Agatha, who had arched her back and hissed when Garrett brought him into the room.

"Play nice," Garrett said to Blackbeard as he set him on his perch.

"Does Blackbeard seem okay to you?" I asked Garrett after I handed him a cup of coffee.

"He seems fine to me. Why do you ask?"

"It's just that while you were in the senior home he was such a chatterbox, but I've barely heard him talk at all in the past couple of weeks."

"Blackbeard only talks if he has something to say. I'm sure if there were a problem, he would let us know. Do we have any fresh cream left?"

I nodded. "I'll get it."

"What are your plans for the day?" Garrett asked.

"I have some work to do for the paper and then I'm meeting Brooke Johnson for lunch. She wants me to help out with the Spring Fling."

"I always look forward to that."

I refilled my coffee cup and sat down at the table. "It'll be my first year on the island in April. What sort of things can I expect?"

"They hold a street fair downtown over a three-day weekend. Crafters from all over come to sell their wares. There's also a music festival with different bands playing on a bandstand erected in the town square. Oh, and the food; the food is my favorite part."

"I love street fair food," I replied. "Bratwurst, kettle corn, chili fries."

"The food is pretty spectacular, but the biggest draw is the parade on Saturday, which features local dogs and cats either being pulled in carts, walked on leashes, or riding on floats. Blackbeard and I used to ride on the float sponsored by the veterinary hospital before I ended up in this darn chair."

"I don't see why you couldn't still ride on the float as long as you had a secure place to sit. I think

I'll talk to Jack about taking Kizzy. It sounds like a lot of fun."

"What sounds like fun?" George asked as he entered through the back door.

Garrett explained about the Spring Fling while I took the muffins out of the oven. Once breakfast was served we all settled in to eat. Afterward, I cleaned the kitchen, and then went upstairs to file my articles. While I was at it, I checked the newspaper email and sent a few responses. I sent Jack a quick message, filling him in on what I had done, and logged off the computer. I still had two hours before I needed to meet Brooke. I felt like I should be working on the Bobby Boston investigation, but I wasn't sure what to do next. We had several working theories going, and Rick and Quinten were both looking in to things. Neither, I was certain, needed my help.

I stood up from my seat behind my desk and walked over to the window. I tried to picture exactly how things had played out on the day Bobby died. I now knew he had been at work but had gone home early. I still wanted to know why. If there was a killer, had Bobby been lured home by him? I could imagine a situation where Bobby received a message that something was wrong with Abby or one of the kids. In that event, he would rush home to help. He might also have left early because he wasn't feeling well, or maybe his replacement came in early, so he decided to head home.

I had to assume that if Bobby had been murdered, the killer must have been waiting at the house, which meant he'd known Abby and the kids weren't home. I walked across the room and took a notepad and pen off my desk. I wrote down a few ideas: find out why

Bobby went home early, and find out who knew Abby wasn't at home. The more I thought about it, the more it seemed whoever set things up for Bobby's murder must have been close to him, not some random arsonist trying to divert attention from himself.

I walked back to the window, taking the pad with me this time. Somehow, looking outside helped to clarify my mind. I tried to picture the series of events that took place to understand what must have happened. Bobby left work early and headed home. He probably used a remote to open the garage door and then drove inside. Someone must have been waiting either in the garage, in the house, or outside, because logic would dictate that someone must have approached the car, causing Bobby to roll down the window before unbuckling his seat belt, and probably before turning off the engine, although the killer could certainly have restarted it.

Once Bobby rolled down the window, the killer forced a rag with chloroform or some other anesthetizing agent over his mouth, knocking him out. He closed the garage door and left until Bobby was dead. I wondered how long a person rendered unconscious by chloroform remained unconscious, and how long it took to die of carbon monoxide poisoning delivered by a running vehicle in an enclosed space. The more I thought about it, the odder the whole thing seemed. I didn't have all the facts, but it seemed trying to kill someone with car exhaust was probably a lengthy process. Seemed like a risky way to kill him when Abby could have come home at any time.

The more I thought about that, the more I accepted I didn't have the background to theorize what might have occurred or the time line necessary to kill Bobby. My best bet was to try to figure out what time Bobby left the firehouse, what time Abby found him, and whether Bobby could have died from the exhaust in the enclosed garage in the time between the two events.

I didn't have a lot of time left before I needed to meet Brooke. I took Kizzy out for a bathroom break and decided to make a quick stop at the firehouse. When I got there, I was greeted by a very nice man who introduced himself as Kyle. I asked if he had known Bobby and he nodded. As it turned out, they had worked together right before Bobby had died.

"I'm trying to help Abby with the insurance company, and any details I can find out about his death would really help," I said.

"What would you like to know?"

"I understand Bobby was on shift the day he died."

"That's correct."

"And he was due to get off at five but left early for some reason."

Kyle nodded. "That's also true."

"Do you remember what time he left and why he left early?"

Kyle tapped his chin with his index finger. "I guess he must have left at about two. He'd been upstairs in the little room we use as an office, filing reports. He came down complaining of a headache, and the captain told him he could take off. Sam was working the shift after us and agreed to come in early."

"Other than the headache, how did Bobby seem that day?" I asked.

"What do you mean?"

"Did he seem agitated? Depressed? Like a man who was about to end his life?"

Kyle shook his head. "Not at all. Like I said, he had a headache, so I guess he was dragging a bit, but he certainly didn't seem suicidal. I told the investigator that when we spoke, but he didn't seem to think it was important."

"Do you remember the 911 call coming in?"

"I sure do. Talk about a shock."

"And what time was that?" I asked.

"I guess around three o'clock. The official time will be in the report."

"So the call came in and your crew responded. Were you the first ones there?"

"Captain Oliver was there. He was the one who told us that Bobby was dead. That he had killed himself. We're a family around here, so it was a real tough day for everyone."

"Yes, I imagine it was. I'm sure it's hard for you to talk about it, and I do appreciate you giving me a few minutes of your time." I stood up from the bench I was seated on and turned to leave. "By the way, if the firehouse receives a call for medical assistance, who responds?"

"The whole team. We're a unit. Where one man goes, we all go."

"Do you remember receiving a medical emergency call between the time Bobby left and the time you received the 911 call regarding his death?"

"No. It was a quiet day. Completely uneventful until the call about Bobby came through."

I left the firehouse and drove to Gertie's to meet Brooke.

As I had begun to suspect, the time line that had been presented wasn't lining up for either a suicide or a murder by exhaust. Abby was out shopping the day Bobby died. He came home early but had been expected at five, so even if Abby hadn't known he was going to be early, it stood to reason she would be home before five herself. Because neither Bobby, in the case of suicide, or the killer, in the case of murder, knew exactly when Abby would be home, it seemed a more efficient form of death, such as a gunshot to the head, would have been a quicker and more reliable method of achieving the final objective.

"Sorry I'm late," I said to Brooke, who was already seated in a booth when I arrived.

"No problem at all. I only just got here myself. I ordered us sweet tea. Gertie said she'd be back to get our order in a minute. You look winded. Did you hurry over here from somewhere?"

"I was at the firehouse speaking to a very nice man named Kyle about the day Bobby died. I'm not really winded, just flustered."

"Oh. And why is that?"

"The more information I gather, the more certain I am that something is off. Did you know Bobby had been on shift at the firehouse on the day he died?"

Brooke lifted a brow. "No. I didn't realize that. Do you think it's relevant?"

I shook a packet of sugar, then poured it into my already sweet tea. "I think it is. Abby told me that Bobby wasn't due home until five. She came home at around three with her groceries, planning to put the food away and then go pick up the kids in time to get home to make dinner at five. When she arrived, she smelled exhaust. She went into the garage, found Bobby dead, and called 911. Kyle told me that Bobby left early because he had a headache. Even if he drove straight home, he couldn't have arrived until two-fifteen. He must have realized Abby wasn't there even before getting out of his car because hers would have been missing, but it doesn't seem he could have known when she would get home. Does it make sense that he would spontaneously decide to close the garage door but not turn off the car engine?"

Brooke shook her head. "No. It doesn't seem like a decision he would make. Even if he'd suffered some weird impulse to end his life, he wouldn't want to risk Abby finding him after he passed out but before he died."

"I agree. And I did some checking: with modern catalytic converters, death by exhaust can take an extended period of time. I know Abby has a two-car garage, so there was a lot of space to be filled by the exhaust. It seems Bobby would have known that and realized he didn't have time to give in to his impulse, supposing he even had one."

"Yeah, and what about the note? The note makes it sound like he planned his suicide, that it wasn't an impulse."

I drummed my fingers on the table. "Even if Bobby didn't kill himself, if someone knocked him out and set him up to die of exhaust fumes, it seems like the time line is too tight. Abby said when she got home she could smell the exhaust, but most of it had dissipated from the garage."

"What are you saying?" Brooke asked.

"I'm saying it wasn't exhaust delivered by a car in a garage that killed Bobby."

"So what did?"

"I don't know," I admitted. I thought about what I knew. Quinten had said no drugs or alcohol were present in Bobby's system, but what about drugs not tested for? Could he have been given something earlier in the day that resulted in a headache? Could whatever he'd been given have made Bobby more sensitive to the exhaust he was exposed to later? I wasn't sure exactly what might have been used to prime the pump, but it seemed it was something worth exploring.

After Brooke and I ordered our lunch, the topic of discussion changed to the upcoming Spring Fling. Brooke shared Garrett's enthusiasm, and the more she spoke about it, the more excited I became to participate. I had the idea of doing some sort of a scavenger hunt. The newspaper could host the event, and a list of places to visit and things to find could be provided for those who wanted to play. Whoever found the most items would be eligible for a prize.

"I love that idea." Brooke beamed. "What kind of items are you thinking of?"

"The goal should be to have the participant visit as many places as possible and attend as many events as they can. We could have each band that plays announce a secret word at some point during their performance. The question on the scavenger hunt sheet could be: What was the secret word for band A or band B or band C? Or we could ask them to tell us the title of the first song played by a particular band. And each booth could have a symbol that must be matched. For example, we could produce a series of symbols that would be featured on a booth. The game will ask the player to identify which booth the cat symbol goes with, etc. There are a lot of ways to accomplish what we're trying to do."

"I love it," Brooke said. "Bring it up at the planning meeting next week. Maybe you can have a sample of what you have in mind."

"I can do that." I glanced down at my phone. "Excuse me; it's Brit. It could be important."

"Go ahead and answer."

I clicked the Answer button and placed the phone to my ear. "What's up?"

"I'm at Abby's. She's having pains. I think I should take her to the ER just to be safe, but the kids are here. I was hoping you could come over. I tried calling Laurie, but she's in the middle of a class."

"I'll be right there."

I hung up and explained that I had to leave but promised to bring everything we'd need to organize the scavenger hunt when I attended the planning meeting the following week. We'd never gotten around to talking about the baby shower, but that would have to wait for another day.

Chapter 10

I brought the kids to the resort rather than waiting with them at Abby's. The girls were unsure about it at first, but then they met Kizzy, Agatha, and Blackbeard. While all the animals were a huge hit, it was Blackbeard who made them laugh by repeating lines he'd picked up from a pirate movie over and over again. If I didn't know better, I'd think the crafty bird understood the situation and knew the kids needed a diversion.

Clara and Garrett were both home when we arrived and were willing to help. George and Vikki came over as soon as they heard what was going on, so we ended up with five adults and three animals to entertain four children. Clara and Garrett were sitting at the card table playing a game with the girls, while Vikki read a book to the twins. George sat near Vikki, seemingly as interested in the story as the three-year-olds. It appeared they were well occupied and having a wonderful time, so I brought my laptop downstairs and began to work on a few ideas I'd been mulling over.

I remembered Quinten had said that according to the ME's report, Bobby had a small bruise on his upper lip. He thought he could have received it when the killer, had there been one, held a chloroform-soaked rag over Bobby's mouth to render him unconscious before asphyxiating him in the car. At first, I believed a rag over the mouth followed with a garage filled with exhaust was exactly what had happened, but what if the item placed over Bobby's mouth was something else entirely? On a hunch, I Googled the suspect who had just popped into my head. After pulling up past and present news items relating to my suspect, I focused on one particular article and gasped.

I glanced into the living room once again and confirmed that everyone was still happy and occupied. I picked up my phone and headed into the kitchen. I dialed Quinten's phone number and waited, hoping he'd pick up.

"Davenport."

"Hi, Quinten, it's Jill. Do you have a moment to chat?"

"Absolutely. What's on your mind?"

I sat down at the kitchen table where I could keep an eye on the group in the living room without being overheard. "I've been thinking about the series of events leading up to Bobby's death. The time line seems all wrong whichever theory we go with." I proceeded to go over the entire time line, from Bobby leaving the firehouse to Abby finding him in the car. I expressed my opinion that it didn't seem as if there'd been enough time for the garage-filled-with-exhaust theory to work. Quinten agreed with my assessment.

"Other than car exhaust, are there other ways to deliver a lethal amount of carbon monoxide?" I asked.

"Sure. Quite a few, in fact."

"Is there a way carbon monoxide can be condensed and delivered more directly, say via an air tank?"

"You're thinking someone used an air tank filled with carbon monoxide to deliver a fatal dose in a short amount of time?"

"It's an idea. You did say the coroner noted a bruise on Bobby's upper lip. Could it have been created by an oxygen mask being held against his face?"

"I didn't see the bruise myself, so I can't say for sure, but it makes sense that the bruise could have been created by an oxygen mask being forcefully held against his face."

"I have some new information that's made me believe that's what may have occurred. I'd like to discuss it with you and Rick. Are you free this afternoon?"

"I can be."

"Okay. I'll call Rick and get back to you."

I texted Brit to see how things were going. Abby had seen a nurse and was waiting to see a doctor. Brit wasn't sure how long that would take. I assured her the kids were well attended and having a good time and welcome to stay here for as long as need be. Then I called Rick to ask if it would be okay for Quinten and me to come by. He said he had time to speak to us, so I arranged to meet him in half an hour. I motioned for George to join me in the kitchen and explained what was going on, and he assured me that he would take charge of the kids until I returned.

******

The first thing I did when I arrived at Rick's office was ask him if he had a list of the employees at the cleaning service. He handed it to me. I looked at it, then made eye contact with both men. "I think I know what happened."

"Care to share?" Rick asked.

I nodded. "Bear with me as I work through this in some sort of a logical fashion."

They were comfortable with my proceeding at my own pace.

"The first thing that happened," I began, "was that Pop Seaton's boat burned. At the time you," I glanced at Rick, "believed he may have set the fire to collect the insurance money. He had an expensive policy he'd been paying on for years. He couldn't collect on it because the policy didn't cover natural wear and tear, and the boat was dry-docked. After the boat burned, Pop was able to file a claim and now has a newer boat from which to conduct his fishing business."

I paused and prepared to make my next point. "The theory was a good one despite the fact that Pop was off the island at the time of the fire. You continued to pursue that angle until the second fire occurred, at which time you were forced to take a closer look at your assumptions. By the time the third, fourth, and fifth fires occurred, Pop was off the hook, and the culprit, it seemed, was a serial arsonist."

I waited to make sure both men were following me. "As it turned out, the fire that destroyed Pop's boat not only helped him but someone else benefited as well. I spoke to one of the men at the firehouse, who confirmed that the fire department was looking at cutting two positions, decreasing the three-man teams to two men on the overnight shifts. Bobby and Sam, the most recently hired men, were the ones who would have been laid off. Captain Oliver used the fire on Pop's boat to argue that a hot and deadly fire could occur at any time of the day or night and the cuts shouldn't be made. The immediate reaction by the higher-ups was that the fire was an isolated incident. Of course, by the time all five structures had burned, talk of personnel cuts were off the table."

Rick and Quinten glanced at each other. I think they were catching on as to where I was going with this.

"What if," I continued, "Pop did burn his boat for the very reason you suspected he did in the first place, to collect the insurance money? I know he was out of town, but he could have set everything up and then used a timer to ignite the blaze, or maybe he hired someone to do it for him. Meanwhile, Captain Oliver was looking at personnel cuts and realized the fire was a godsend, providing him with the perfect argument he needed to maintain his workforce at the present level. The people in charge considered the boat to be an isolated incident, so Captain Oliver got the idea to set a second fire and then a third."

"Why would Oliver do something like that?" Rick asked. "He must have had to deal with layoffs in the past."

"He did," I confirmed. "I found an article about a fire in Georgia in which two men died. The deaths were not only tragic but controversial, because the men worked for a large fire department that used four-man teams to handle structures with multiple stories. As a cost-cutting measure, the teams had been reduced to three men each, and it was demonstrated that the probable cause of the death of the two firefighters was the fact that there weren't enough men to effectively tackle the blaze." I looked at each man in the room. "The third man on the three-man team, the one who survived, was Captain Oliver, before he was a captain and before he moved to the island."

"So Captain Oliver suffered the loss of his teammates in a horrible incident in his past, which he possibly believed could have been prevented if the teams hadn't been cut," Rick began. "When talk of cuts to his own teams came down the pike, he remembered his past experience and maybe went a little over the edge."

"Possibly," I agreed.

"So what does the list from the cleaning service and Bobby Boston's death have to do with any of this?" Rick asked.

"The arsonist chose well insured and completely vacant properties where the owner was out of town. The question as to how the arsonist knew who was going to be out of town has been brought up in previous discussions. When the woman with the art studio mentioned the cleaning service, and then the man with the barn said he used the same service, it occurred to me the service could be the key. As it turns out, the local Merry Maids franchise is owned by Melissa Petrie."

"Why does that name sound familiar?" Quinten asked.

"Sam Petrie is the second firefighter who would have been laid off. My theory is that Captain Oliver went to the two men who had the most to lose if the layoffs occurred and asked for their help with the fires. Sam's wife had access not only to the comings and goings of property owners on the island but, in many cases, to the homes themselves. It wouldn't be hard for a maid with a key to a house to snoop around in private files while the owner was away."

"Files such as insurance policies," Quinten said.

"Exactly."

Rick leaned back in his chair and steepled his fingers, then he rocked gently back and forth as he appeared to be taking a minute to process things. "Okay, so far I follow," he said. "Pop burns down his boat for the insurance money, giving Captain Oliver the idea of creating future business for his crew as some sort of an insurance policy against layoffs, which he'd had a bad experience with in the past. He brought Sam and Bobby into his confidence, because he figured he'd need help and they had the most to lose. Sam's wife got the information relating to insurance policies and out-of-town trips that helped them to pick their targets. Everything was going according to plan until a house that was supposed to be vacant was actually occupied, and a man died. Bobby is guilt ridden at the death of this man, so he kills himself?"

"I think you have it up to the end," I responded. "It does seem Bobby had a motive to commit suicide, but after taking a close look at things, I don't think that's what happened."

Rick leaned forward and placed his forearms on his desk. "Okay. What do you think happened?"

"I think that after the man died in the fire, Bobby was riddled with guilt. I think he went to Captain Oliver and Sam and told them that because a man had died, they needed to go to the authorities and tell them what they'd done. At that point, Bobby became a liability in the eyes of his partners in crime. A plan was hatched to get Bobby and what he knew out of the way." I took a breath. "On the day he was murdered, Bobby was at work. He was tasked with working in a small office by himself, filing incident reports. He came down with a headache, a headache I believe may have been intentionally caused by a leaky heater or some other mode of putting a low level of carbon monoxide into the air. Bobby complained to his teammates about the headache and Sam offered to come in early so Bobby could go home. I'm not sure how Oliver knew Abby wasn't home; maybe Bobby mentioned it at some point.

"Anyway, Bobby drove home and pulled into the garage, where he was met by Oliver. He rolled down his window to ask why the captain was there, and Oliver forced a mask over his face that was filled not with oxygen but with a concentrated form of carbon monoxide. Bobby was dead within minutes. Oliver closed the garage door so enough exhaust would leak into the enclosed space to create the illusion of suicide. Then he put the note in the car, turned off the engine, and left. Abby came home and found Bobby, and called 911, and Oliver, who had been waiting nearby, showed up first so he could control the situation. Oliver told Abby he'd been in the neighborhood due to a medical emergency call, which was how he was able to show up so fast. I checked; there were no medical emergency calls on the day Bobby died. Furthermore, Abby remembered seeing green paint around the dent on her mailbox, and Captain Oliver drives a green SUV."

"Wow; that's quite a theory," Quinten said with a tone of admiration in his voice.

Rick didn't answer right away.

"Rick?" I asked.

"I agree your theory is a good one that makes sense, but how do we prove it?"

"We'll need physical proof or a confession," Quinten added.

"I think I have a really bad idea," I said.

Chapter 11

The first thing I did after explaining my idea to Rick and Quinten was to call Brit. "How's Abby doing?"

"I think she's going to be okay. Her blood pressure is high, so they want to keep her overnight. I was just going to call you so we could work out something for the kids."

"They're doing fine at the resort. There are a ton of empty guest rooms on the second floor, so they can stay with me. I'll call George to let him know what we're doing and stop by to pick up some jammies for the kids. Before I do that, though, I need you to do something for me."

"Sure; anything."

"Is Abby's phone nearby?"

"Yes," Brit answered. "She was assigned to a room, where I'm waiting for her. She's having some tests done right now, but the phone is sitting on the table next to the bed."

"I need you to send a text from Abby's phone to a number I'll give you. I'll explain everything later, but I need you to word the text exactly as I say."

Brit did as I asked. A few minutes later, she replied, "It's all set."

"Great. Keep me updated on Abby's condition. I'll call you when it's done."

I clicked off my phone, then looked at Rick. "It looks like we're on."

I called George to let him know the kids were going to be spending the night, and then Quinten, Rick, and I got into my car and headed to Abby's house to put my plan into action.

I'd had Brit text Captain Oliver from Abby's phone, telling him she knew about the fires he'd set because Bobby had told her what was going on before his death. She hadn't said anything to anyone yet because Bobby had asked her not to, but she was desperate to pay her mortgage so she and the kids wouldn't be thrown out on the street, and she figured her silence must be worth something. She added that Bobby had left a file locked in his desk at the house that she knew contained the proof he'd been gathering. She was willing to give Oliver the file in exchange for ten thousand dollars. Captain Oliver texted back agreeing to the meeting. I planned to show up as Abby's representative, at which time I hoped to squeeze a confession out of him. Rick and Quinten would be listening in.

The closer we got to Abby's house, the harder my heart pounded. By the time we pulled into her driveway, my hands were sweating so badly I could barely get my seat belt off. Quinten dropped Rick and me off, then went off to listen from a safe distance.

He was our safety net, in case things didn't go according to plan.

The first thing we did was go into Bobby's office. We used photos from police reports, along with props like thumb drives to create a file, which I had to convince Captain Oliver contained enough evidence to blow his arson spree wide open. Rick placed a listening device in my ear and a wire under my sweater to record our conversation. Hopefully, Oliver wouldn't show up with a gun, intending to shoot first and ask questions later.

We weren't sure if Sam Petrie knew Oliver had killed Bobby. We knew he'd come in to cover Bobby's shift when he left, so he wasn't the one to do the deed, but he may very well have been in on the plan. We hoped Oliver would provide the missing pieces to put this mystery to bed.

I left the front door of the house open, with a note telling him to come in. Rick wanted Oliver in the office where he was waiting, just on the other side of the wall in the bedroom, so the note also said Captain Oliver should come back to the office when he arrived. I took a seat behind the desk and waited. My heart was pounding so loudly by the time I heard the front door open that I wondered if Rick and Quinten could hear it through the listening pieces.

"Take a deep breath and try to relax," Rick whispered in my ear after someone—we assumed Oliver—entered through the front door. "Confidence is key. Don't let him see you sweat."

I wanted to assure Rick I had this and he could relax, but in that moment, I was too scared to speak. I nodded, which was ridiculous because Rick could hear but not see me.

"What are you doing here?" Captain Oliver asked when he stood in the office doorway.

"Abby's very pregnant, and the stress of everything was getting to her, so I agreed to fill in."

Captain Oliver took a step into the doorway. "Do you have the envelope?"

I nodded. "I do. Do you have the money?"

"I have it. I'm going to need to see the envelope first. For all I know, Abby is lying about having any sort of proof I set those fires."

I held up the envelope, which was filled with random items that looked a lot like they might be proof but in actuality were nothing of the kind. "The proof is real. I think in some part of his mind, Bobby never did trust you. He knew the plan you concocted was a risk, and he wanted to be sure that she had something to negotiate with should she need it."

"Can I see the file?" Oliver held out his hand.

"Not until you show me the money."

Oliver hesitated. I could see he wasn't completely buying the whole thing, but he was uncertain enough not to walk away.

"You know, if you'd figured out some way to get rid of Bobby that didn't look like a suicide, you could have prevented this," I said. "Abby would have gotten the insurance money she needed to raise the kids and she wouldn't need to use the file as leverage to get the money to pay her mortgage."

Captain Oliver took a step toward me. He held out his hand. "I think I've had enough of this little charade. Hand over the file before I have to hurt you too."

"Hand over the money first," I insisted, in a tone of voice that sounded a lot more confident than I was feeling.

Captain Oliver pulled a gun out of his pocket. He pointed it at my chest before taking several steps forward and grabbing the envelope from me. "I'm sorry to have to do this."

In the next moment, everything went black.

******

I wrinkled my nose at the god-awful smell.

"Come on, honey. Time to wake up."

I slowly opened my eyes. Quinten was hovering over me with something in his hand that he had been waving under my nose. "What happened?"

"I'm afraid Oliver clocked you before Rick could respond."

I put my hand to my head, where a huge bump was beginning to form. The bastard must have hit me with the gun. I suppose I should be glad he hadn't shot me, but my head was pounding too loudly to be glad of much of anything. "Did he get away?"

"Rick caught up with him before he even got out of the house." Quinten held out a hand and pulled me to my feet. I swayed a bit as a wave of dizziness gripped me. "I'm going to take you to the emergency room to have your head looked at. Rick will be tied up for a while."

"I'm fine," I said, trying to focus on something solid to make the room stop spinning.

Quinten put an arm around my waist. "You'll probably be fine, but when it comes to head injuries it's better safe than sorry."

I could hear the sound of talking in the distance as Quinten led me through the house toward the back door. We'd left my car on the street behind Abby's so Captain Oliver wouldn't see it when he arrived. Quinten helped me into the passenger seat and then went around to the driver's side. He opened the door and slipped inside.

"Did we get what we need to prove Bobby was murdered?" I asked.

"I think we did." Quinten started the engine and pulled away from the curb. "It was a brave thing you did to help your friend."

"I don't know if it was brave or foolish, but I do hope we have enough evidence to get the insurance company to pay her the money she has coming to her. I can't imagine how difficult it must be to try to move forward with everything she has to deal with."

"She has had more than her share of grief and worry to deal with, but I think with friends like you and Brit, she'll come through this just fine."

I leaned my head back against the seat and closed my eyes. I couldn't remember ever having such a bad headache in my entire life.

After we arrived at the hospital, Quinten turned me over to the ER staff after promising to wait for me. As far as I was concerned, I'd let them check me out and then I planned to go home, and I'd need someone to drive me. Luckily, the ER wasn't all that busy, so I got to see a doctor right away. He determined I had only a mild concussion and would be able to go home, as I'd hoped. I was waiting for the discharge paperwork when Brit poked her head in.

"Oh my God, what happened?" Brit asked.

"Apparently, Captain Oliver wasn't all that thrilled at my blackmail attempt." I put a hand to my head. "I'm fine, though, and I'm pretty sure we have what we need to prove he killed Bobby."

Brit frowned. "I want to say that's wonderful, but all I can really come up with is that's terrible. I'm having a hard time with the fact that Bobby's killer turned out to be a man he liked and respected."

"Yeah, it's pretty sad," I agreed. "I guess the man came up with a really bad idea during a moment of desperation, and the deeper he got, the more convoluted it became. The thing is, if a man hadn't died in that last fire, the spree would most likely have just ended, Bobby and Sam would have been able to keep their jobs, and Captain Oliver would have been able to retain his crew, and no one would be all that much worse off than they were when the arsons began. Even the owner of the home where the man died is getting a brand-new house to replace the money pit that burned to the ground." I winced slightly as I tried to stand. I was going to need to take it easy for a few hours. "How's Abby doing?"

"The nurse I spoke to seemed to think she'll be fine," Brit answered. "They want to keep her a day or two, but she should be able to come home if they can get her blood pressure down. She's very grateful you're watching after the kids."

"Technically, it's your uncle, Vikki, and Clara who are watching them now, but I know they're happy to do it. Tell Abby not to worry about a thing. They can stay with us as long as necessary."

By the time Quinten dropped me off at home, the house was quiet. George and Vikki were sitting in the living room talking, but I didn't see evidence of

Garrett, Clara, or any of the children. "Where is everyone?" I asked.

"Sleeping," Vikki said. "The kids were all pretty wiped out, so we put them to bed. Garrett and Clara went to their rooms shortly after that. If I had to guess, I'd say everyone will be out for the duration. I planned to sleep in my old room on the second floor, so I could listen for the kids should they wake up."

"That's very nice of you, but I can just move downstairs," I offered.

"No," Vikki said, rising to her feet. "You've had a head injury and need to get some rest. I'm going to run over to my cabin to grab a few things and then I'll be back."

My head was pounding, and I wanted to try to sleep it off, so I didn't argue. Besides, Vikki seemed to have more color in her face and spunk in her step than I'd seen in weeks. I hoped that meant she was feeling better about the decision she had to make.

"I'll wait for Vikki if you want to head on up," George offered.

"Thanks. I guess I will." I glanced around the room. "Where's Kizzy?"

"Sleeping with the girls. I took her out before we put them all to bed, so I think she'll be fine. The kids seem to love her and she seems to love them, so I didn't think you'd mind if she slept in their room. I think her presence has brought a certain amount of comfort to all four children."

"I'm fine with her sleeping with them. And thank you. For everything."

"I was happy to help. It's been a while since I spent any real time with the under-twelve crowd. I actually had a very good time."

I smiled. "I'm glad. I guess I'll head up. I'll see you in the morning. Tell Vikki if she needs help with the kids during the night, she can wake me."

"I'll tell her, but I think she'll be fine. She has a very natural way with kids. I never thought of her as being the type to settle down and have children of her own, but after watching her with them today, I think it would be a shame if she didn't."

"Yeah," I said as a feeling of sorrow for Vikki and her situation gripped my heart. "It really would be."

Chapter 12

Saturday, January 27

Surprisingly enough, I got a really good night's sleep and woke feeling headache-free and refreshed in the morning. I headed downstairs to look for Kizzy, but she was no longer sleeping in the room with the two older girls. I could hear someone in the kitchen, so I headed in that direction.

"You look better," Vikki greeted me.

"I feel better." I glanced at Kizzy, who had trotted over to greet me. "Has she been out?"

"I took her out when I got up," Vikki confirmed. "Coffee?"

"I'd love some, but I can get it." I headed to the counter where the coffeemaker was kept. "Have you been up long?"

"About an hour. I figured the kids will be awake soon, so I should try to get in a little bit of me time before they get up."

I poured my coffee and had a seat at the table. "I really appreciate you taking care of them yesterday. I know Abby appreciates it as well."

"Honestly," Vikki said, wrapping her hands around her mug, "it was my pleasure. Not only did I have a wonderful time, but I think spending time with the kids has helped me with my own problem as well."

I raised a brow. "And how is that?"

"They helped me realize I really do want to have children of my own if it's at all possible, and I'm not ready to give up on the idea quite yet. When I was looking at the decision before, it was more about Rick and his desire to have children. It's too early to tell if our relationship will stand the test of time and I didn't want a decision regarding children to put undue stress on a relationship that hasn't progressed to that point yet. But with the realization that I want children for me, whether they're with Rick or not, I've come to the conclusion I'm going to talk to my doctor about treatment options that will keep that door open. At least for now."

I smiled. "That's great. I'm glad you were able to come up with something you're comfortable with."

"Oh, by the way," Vikki added, "Nicole is home. Kizzy headed straight to her cabin when I took her out this morning. I cringed when Kizzy scratched at her door, but she opened it, saw the puppy, and a huge smiled crossed her face. She actually got down on her knees and gave her a very enthusiastic greeting."

"You're kidding." I'd never seen Nicole greet a human with that degree of enthusiasm. "Did she say where she'd been?"

"I mentioned we'd been concerned about her, and she said she'd been away on a research trip for a few days. She hadn't been aware she'd left the light on and apologized for any inconvenience. She even wished me a good day after I headed back to the main house with Kizzy."

I got up to pour myself a second cup of coffee. "Maybe there's hope for her yet. She's the only long-term tenant who hasn't shown any inclination to be part of the community, and I have to confess that I feel bad that we naturally exclude her."

"I'm not sure she's ready to join the family quite yet, but she does seem a bit more receptive." Vikki glanced at the clock. "I'm going to run back to my place to shower. I told the kids we'd go into town to buy Abby a get-well-soon gift. I should be back before they crawl out of bed, but if I'm not, tell them that I didn't forget and will be back shortly."

Kizzy came over and put her head in my lap after Vikki left. I scratched her behind the ears for a few minutes before getting up and going to the refrigerator. I could hear Clara moving around in her room and knew Garrett would be up soon as well. I supposed I should figure out what to make for breakfast. With the kids in the house, it felt even more like a family. Nicole was home and Vikki seemed to have worked through her decision. Bobby's killer was in jail and Abby should be able to collect the insurance money. Now all I needed for my equilibrium to be restored was to have Jack back in my daily life.

******

George had decided to go with Vikki to take the kids shopping, Garrett and Clara were watching reruns of an old soap opera they both enjoyed, and Brit had gone to see Abby, so I made a list and headed to the grocery store while everyone appeared to be occupied. I didn't know for certain whether the kids would still be with us at dinnertime, but I suspected they would be, so I decided to make a big pot of spaghetti with garlic bread and salad. Most kids liked spaghetti, and so far, it seemed Abby's four weren't picky eaters, which made things a lot easier. I remembered going through food phases when I was a kid. At one point I would only eat peanut butter sandwiches and macaroni and cheese. That was it. Nothing else, other than sweets, that is. When I got a little older I went through a salad phase. If a rabbit or a turtle wouldn't eat what had been placed on my plate, I wouldn't either.

I was checking the spice rack for the items I'd need for the sauce when my phone rang. It was Brit. "Are you at the hospital?"

"I am."

"And how's Abby today?" I added a few more items to my list.

"Better. The doctor said he'd consider letting her go home, but he's concerned about releasing her to take care of four children without help. He told me that he's worried she'd end up undoing everything he did to stabilize her blood pressure. I was thinking I might go stay with her for a few days at least."

I opened the pantry and checked for tomato sauce. "Why don't you have her come here? The kids are settled in and having a blast with their honorary aunts and uncles, and we have another empty room right next to the one the twins have been using. She can get the rest she needs and still spend time with the kids."

"Are you sure?"

"Positive. I'm sure the others will be fine with it as well. In fact, maybe she should plan to stay with us until the baby is born. Once she's here, we can help her make more permanent arrangements. Maybe we can help her find a nanny or something."

I could hear Brit talking to someone in the background.

"I gotta go," Brit said. "The doctor wants to talk to me about Abby's limitations. I think having her stay with us until the baby is born is a wonderful idea. I'll run it past her and the doctor and let you know for sure."

I had just hung up with Brit and was getting ready to take Kizzy out when I heard the doorbell. "I wonder who that could be?" I asked the puppy, who had already taken off running toward the front of the house. I told Kizzy to stay, then opened the door to find a deliveryman with a huge bouquet of flowers.

"Are you Jill Hanford?" the man asked.

"I am."

He handed me the large arrangement. "These are for you, then."

I accepted the flowers. "Thank you so much. Hang on while I grab a tip."

"The tip has been taken care of."

"Okay, then, have a wonderful day."

The flowers, as I suspected, were from Jack. There was a card attached that said, *I'm sorry for everything. Have dinner with me.*

I set the flowers on the table and dialed Jack's number. "Thank you; they're beautiful."

"I'm glad you like them and again, I'm so sorry. For everything."

"Is your mom gone?" I asked.

"She left this morning."

"And...?" I almost hated to ask.

"And I made sure she understood that my life is on Gull Island now and I'd be cutting back on my fiction output. I don't want to give it up entirely because I really do love the creative outlet, but I think I'm going to limit myself to one, maybe two books a year. There was a time I would have taken every opportunity presented to me, but I think that time has passed."

I leaned a hip on the counter. "Was she upset?"

"She was, but she'll get over it. I suggested she might want to take on another writer. She really is an excellent agent. I'm sure there are new writers out there who would welcome her enthusiasm. I'm not sure she was totally sold on the idea, but she seems to be considering it. So, how about dinner? I've missed you."

"I'd love to, but Abby's four kids are staying with us while she's in the hospital. I'm making spaghetti. You're welcome to join us if you'd like."

"I'd like that very much. Is Abby okay?"

"She will be. She had a few pains and her blood pressure was up, so the doctor is keeping an eye on her. George and Vikki took the kids shopping and I was about to head out to the grocery store to pick up some things I'll need for dinner."

"It's nice of you and the gang to help Abby out with the kids. I'm sure she really appreciates it. How are things going with the Bobby Boston case?"

"Solved. I'll fill you in when you get here."

After I hung up the phone, I started out to the grocery store. If the kids were staying with us for the long term, I figured I'd better pick up kid-friendly food like cereal, peanut butter, macaroni and cheese, and apple slices. I didn't think they had any food allergies, so I tossed in string cheese, bananas, and fruit cups as well. By the time I reached the checkout counter my basket was almost overflowing with everything I hoped we'd need.

"Looks like you're planning to feed an army," Brooke said as she slipped into line behind me. "A kid army, I'd say."

"Abby's kids are staying at the resort while she's in the hospital."

"Abby's still in the hospital? What happened?"

"Just some random pains and high blood pressure. I think she'll be getting out today or tomorrow. Brit's looking in to having her stay with us at the resort until the baby's born."

Brooke hugged me. "That's very sweet and thoughtful. The community really lucked out when you decided to move here."

I tried not to blush. "Thanks. The gang and I are happy to help."

"What can I do?" Brooke asked. "Do we need to organize a fund-raiser? Line up babysitters? We never did settle on the details for that baby shower."

I explained very briefly that we'd managed to uncover the truth behind Bobby's death and it looked like Abby would be getting her insurance money, which would be enough to pay off her debts and hire some part-time help. I thought the baby shower was an excellent idea. Brooke agreed to call me so we could talk about the specifics of both the shower and our investigation. When I first met her, I'd actually suspected her of being a killer. In the months I'd known her, I'd counted myself lucky again and again that in that instance, my instinct had been wrong.

******

"Who wants more garlic bread?" I asked later that evening, after the entire writer family had gathered for a communal meal. Not only had Abby been released to come and stay with us, but the kids were excited to be able to stay with Kizzy, Blackbeard, Agatha, and all their honorary aunts and uncles.

"I do," Alex said, raising his hand.

"Me too," George agreed.

I took a piece and passed the basket around the table. We'd seated the kids so they each had at least one adult sitting next to them in the event they needed help with serving or cutting. The oldest of the four, Rachael, was seated between Rick and Vikki, both of whom were doting on her, while Rebecca enjoyed her own brand of attention from Alex and Brit. I hadn't expected anyone from the retreat to have a problem with the kids being here, but it seemed that not only were we helping them, they were helping us by bringing a new, youthful energy to the table. I was really looking forward to them being with us for a couple of months.

After the meal was over, Abby went upstairs to rest, and I took Kizzy out. I was glad Jack grabbed a jacket to join me.

"Your dinner was delicious," he said, kissing me on the cheek as I opened the back door and then stepped aside for Kizzy to rush out.

"Thanks. It was a fun dinner. It seemed like everyone was enjoying having kids at the table."

"They're great kids. Did you know Timmy already knows the entire alphabet? Not too bad at all for a three-year-old. And Tommy can count to ten."

I laughed. "You sound like a proud papa."

"Maybe not a papa, but I do like the sound of Uncle Jack."

"Are you an uncle?" I asked.

"No. I'm an only child, so no nieces and nephews. There are times, like tonight, when I wish I had children in my life."

"Do you ever wish you'd married and had children?"

"No," Jack said decisively. "Don't get me wrong; I love kids, and maybe someday I could even see myself wanting to raise one. But my life has been perfect to this point." Jack tilted his head. "Well, almost perfect. The thing is, I like who I've been and who I've become. I wouldn't want to change a thing. How about you? Are you wishing you had a houseful of children of your own?"

I bent down and picked up the stick Kizzy dropped at my feet. "Not really. It's fun having the kids here, but I haven't had to do all that much. I don't think I'd want a houseful to take care of twenty-four-seven. I'd never had to take care of anyone except myself before I moved here. I've enjoyed this time with Kizzy, however. I'm going to miss her when you take her home."

Jack stopped walking. He pulled me into his arms. "You can come and stay with Kizzy and me any time. And when we move into the cabin, we'll see you all the time."

I stood on tiptoe and kissed Jack on the lips. "I'm really glad you decided to stay here on Gull Island with me."

Jack cupped my cheeks with his hands. "I know it may not have seemed like it, but there was never any doubt in my mind that right here with you is where I'll always be."

Chapter 13

Sunday, January 28

Jack had decided to let Kizzy stay with me for a few more days because Abby's children were so firmly attached to her. I knew he missed her, but I could also see he was happy to do anything he could to lighten the burden of the little family. I knew Kizzy would need to go out before any of the children woke up, so I slipped out of bed early, pulled on some warm sweats, and went in search of the agreeable little puppy. Today, she was sleeping on Rachael's bed. It almost seemed like she was taking turns between the four children. After quietly calling Kizzy to my side, we headed down to the first floor of the three-story house. I was heading to the kitchen when I felt something brush my cheek before landing on my shoulder.

"Blackbeard," I screeched. "You scared the living daylights out of me. Whatever are you doing out here?"

I looked toward Garrett's closed bedroom door. He always tucked his bird in for the night before heading in. I was sure he'd done so the previous evening.

"Cabin six, cabin six," Blackbeard said.

"What about cabin six?" I asked.

The current cabin six was occupied by Nicole, although the original had been one of the cabins we'd decided to demolish.

"Cabin six, cabin six," Blackbeard repeated.

"I don't think Nicole would appreciate us dropping in on her at this time of the morning," I informed the bird.

"Walk the dog, walk the dog."

"Yes, I'm going to walk the dog. Do you want to come?" I asked the suddenly talkative bird.

Blackbeard whistled, which usually indicated he wanted whatever you were offering. I tied a tether to his leg so he couldn't fly away, and then Blackbeard, Kizzy, and I went out into the cool morning air. We were just about to pass the trail that veered off to the cabins closest to the marsh when Kizzy barked once and began wagging her tail. I hushed her and then followed her gaze. She seemed to be looking at Nicole, who just happened to be sitting on her front deck.

"Cabin six, cabin six," Blackbeard said.

"All right already." I changed direction. "We'll stop by and say hi to Nicole, but if she snaps at us for coming so early, it's your fault."

Kizzy ran on ahead and we followed.

"Good morning," I called when we got closer.

"You're out early," Nicole said as she bent down to pet Kizzy, who had trotted over to say hi.

"Kizzy needed out. It's a beautiful day but sort of chilly to be sitting out here."

Nicole wrapped her arms around her torso. "It is cold, but I needed to clear my mind. Would you like some coffee?"

Okay, that was new. Yet welcome. "I would. Thank you for asking."

"Let's head inside where it's warmer," Nicole suggested.

"Is it okay if Blackbeard and Kizzy come in?" I asked.

"Certainly. They're welcome any time."

I followed Nicole inside her cabin and took a seat at her dining table. She didn't have a perch for Blackbeard, so I set him on the back of the dining chair next to me. I smiled at Nicole after she set a cup of coffee in front of me.

"I wonder if I can ask you something," Nicole said once she'd taken a seat in the chair across from me.

"Sure. What would you like to know?"

"The Mastermind Group you run. How does it work?"

"We meet once a week, usually on Monday, to chat and discuss whatever project we're working on. If anyone has a mystery they'd like the group to consider helping with, it's at these meetings they bring it up. We're a writers' group, so if there's no mystery that week, we discuss whatever we're writing. Are you interested in joining us?"

"I have a mystery I might be interested in presenting to the group." Nicole sat back in her chair. I could tell by the look on her face that she was uncertain, but it meant a lot that she'd even broached the subject. When she'd first moved in, she'd made it clear she neither needed nor wanted help with anything.

"Why don't you tell me what's on your mind?"

Nicole wet her lips. She folded and then unfolded her arms. She sat forward and then leaned back. Eventually, she began to speak. "The reason I came to the island was to research a missing person. Her name is Emily and she's been missing since last March."

"Is Emily someone you know or someone you're writing about?" I asked.

"Emily is my sister. Half sister, actually. She was just sixteen when she ran away with some boy she met in a bar."

I hadn't been expecting that. "I'm so sorry. You must be so worried about her. Have you heard from her at all?"

Nicole nodded. "At first. First, Emily and I aren't close. She's the product of my mother's second marriage. I was living with a foster family when she was born and am fifteen years older than she is. I care about her, but we don't know each other all that well. The only reason I even knew she'd run away was because she called and told me she was leaving. Apparently, her father had been abusing her and she decided she'd had enough."

I had a million questions, but I felt it would be best to wait for Nicole to fill in the blanks before I started grilling her for more information. Knowing her, that could very well cause her to clam up.

"I tried to talk her into coming to stay with me, but she said she was in love and wanted to start a life with this guy, who I only know as Slayer."

I cringed. Slayer? That didn't sound good.

"Emily knew I was worried about her, so she agreed to send me a selfie once a week to prove she was safe and alive. And she did. Every Monday up until May 15, she sent me a selfie. She looked happy and relaxed in each photo, so I began to worry less. When she missed the fifteenth I wasn't too worried, but when she missed the next week and the next, I got scared. I decided to try to find her, so I went back through the photos, looking for clues. It wasn't easy because the photos had nondescript scenery in the background, but eventually, I caught a break and found one of the places she'd stayed. She'd moved on by the time I found the location where the photo was taken, but I was able to trace her from the next photo based on things she'd said to others I spoke to. I continued to follow the clues until I arrived on Gull Island. The last photo she sent me was this one."

Nicole handed me her phone, which featured a photo of a smiling young girl with long dark hair and shining blue eyes. She was standing in front of a wooden door with the number six on it. "This looks like the door from the one of the old cabins before we remodeled."

"I think it is. Cabin six. The reason I wanted to rent a cabin from you is because my sister's trail died here. When I first contacted you, I hoped your brother would recognize Emily, but then I learned Garrett had already suffered his stroke and was in the hospital this past May. The resort was closed, and I have no way to know if she somehow squatted in the cabin or if she just used it as the backdrop for her photo. By the time I tracked Emily to Gull Island, cabin six—the original cabin six—had already been torn down and any clues that might have existed were long gone."

"Why didn't you say something before this?" I asked.

"Honestly. I didn't trust you. Any of you. The last place my sister was seen was at this resort, and then she simply disappeared. After I got to know everyone, I could see that none of you were responsible for her disappearance. I've exhausted every lead, which were slim to begin with. I need help. I need your help. You and the others. Do you think they'd be willing to take a look at my case?"

I reached across the table and put my hand over Nicole's. "I think they'll be happy to help if they can. You should plan to attend our meeting tomorrow."

Nicole smiled sadly. I hoped we could help her, but a photo of a girl who hadn't been seen for eight months standing in front of a cabin that no longer existed wasn't a lot to go on. Still, if there was anyone who could help Nicole find her sister, it would be our group.

UP NEXT FROM KATHI DALEY BOOKS

Preview

Chapter 1

Wednesday, February 7

"Mornin' Tess, mornin' Tilly," Queenie Samuels greeted my dog Tilly and me. "It looks like a two-bagger today."

I groaned as I accepted two large mail bags from the new postal employee who had recently been hired to help with mail distribution for the White Eagle, Montana, branch of the United States Postal Service. I supposed I should have anticipated the extra workload with Valentine's Day just around the corner.

"Your mom has a package requiring a signature," Queenie informed me. "If you want to sign it out, you can just drop it by her place with the mail to save her the trouble of coming in for it."

I accepted the clipboard and signed my name, Tess Thomas, in the spot reserved for a signature from my mother, Lucy Thomas. I had to admit I was curious about what was in the small box with the foreign postmark.

"The box came from Italy," Queenie informed me as I studied the postmark. "I'm not sure who Romero Montenegro is, but I do love the name. It's so strong and masculine, yet I can't help picturing a half-naked man with dark skin, chiseled features, and dark and soulful eyes every time the name Romero rolls off my tongue."

"You've definitely been reading too many romance novels."

"There's no such thing as reading too many romance novels." Queenie winked.

I opened the top of one of the bags and peered inside. "Did you happen to notice a box for my Aunt Ruthie while you were packing everything up?"

"There was a package. Flat and heavy. I'm thinking a book of some sort."

"It's a photo album. Her son Johnny just had a baby a few weeks ago and Ruthie has her first granddaughter. Johnny promised to send a photo album of baby's first week, and Ruthie has been asking about it every day since she spoke to him. She'll be thrilled it finally arrived." I glanced down at my golden retriever, Tilly. "Are you ready to get started?"

Tilly barked once in reply.

I thanked Queenie and then Tilly and I headed out to my Jeep. Normally, I just parked on one end of Main Street and made my deliveries up one side and down the other. A two-bagger, however, required a slightly different approach; I parked in the middle of the long row of small mom-and-pop-type businesses with the intention of starting in the middle, working one side of the street, crossing, and then doing the other half of the north end, before returning to my Jeep for the second bag and repeating the effort on the south end of town. The diner my mom owned, along with my Aunt Ruthie, was close to the center of town, so I decided to park there and deliver their packages first.

"You're early today," Mom greeted as Tilly and I walked in through the front door at around the same time the breakfast crowd was beginning to disperse.

"Two-bagger."

"Ah. I guess that makes sense. Would you care for some coffee?"

"I don't have time to stay, but I did want to bring you this." I handed my mom the package from Italy.

She looked so completely shocked *and* so completely delighted when I handed it to her that I knew there had been more going on with the foreigner she had met briefly last summer than she was willing to let on.

"Isn't the package from the same man who sent you a card at Christmas?"

"Yes," Mom said, slipping the small package into the large pocket on the front of her apron. "As you know, we met when he was passing through last summer. Since then, we've exchanged correspondence. He's a very nice man I've enjoyed getting to know."

"Queenie said Romero Montenegro sounds like a name belonging to a muscular man with chiseled features and soulful eyes."

Mom quickly glanced away. She picked up a rag and began wiping an already clean counter.

"So, does he have soulful eyes?" I couldn't resist teasing the woman who, as far as I knew, had never even been on a date since she'd been informed my father died fourteen years ago.

"He's a very nice-looking man. Now, if you don't mind, I have customers to see to."

I looked around the half-empty restaurant. Everyone looked to be taken care of, but I didn't argue. I hated it when my brother, Mike, teased me about my love life and I thought it was mean of me to tease Mom about hers. "Ruthie's photo album came. Is she in the kitchen?"

"She is. She'll be thrilled it's finally here." Mom hurried over to the kitchen door and pushed it open. "Ruthie, come on out," Mom called. "Tess is here, and she brought the photo album Johnny sent."

The next twenty minutes were taken up by Ruthie showing Mom and ne, as well as every customer who hadn't managed to escape before she opened the book, photos of little Holly Ruth Turner. She really was cute, but the extra time spent at the diner meant I was going to have to hustle to get my two bags of mail delivered before the shops in the area closed for the day. It was winter in White Eagle, which meant that, except for a few of the restaurants and the bars, the shops in town locked their doors and rolled up the sidewalks by five o'clock.

I managed to make up some time with my next few stops. I tried to pause and chat with a handful of people each day, figuring if I mixed it up I could maintain the relationships I'd built over time without taking a ridiculous amount of time to complete the route assigned to us. Of course, the one stop where I could never seem to get away with a drop and run was the Book Boutique, the bookstore my best friend, Bree Price, owned.

"Oh good, perfect timing," Bree said as I walked through the front door with a large stack of mail. "Wilma was just asking me about the Valentine's Day party Brady's throwing at the shelter."

I smiled at Wilma Cosgrove, White Eagle's new librarian and a fellow dog lover, who had been standing at the counter chatting with Bree. "What do you want to know?"

"I've been thinking of adopting a second dog. Sasha gets bored at home by herself all day, and unlike you, I'm not lucky enough to be able to bring her to work with me. How exactly does the party work?"

I set Bree's mail on the counter. "It's basically an adoption clinic, but Brady has arranged to use the high school's multipurpose room. He's going to decorate it with a Valentine theme and offer punch and cookies to those who show up. He plans to secure the exits other than the main entry, so the dogs and prospective owners can socialize in a casual atmosphere without having to worry about the animals getting out. He even plans to provide bean bag chairs for cuddling, balls for throwing, and toys for playing. He wants folks to relax with and really get to know the dogs available for adoption."

"It sounds like fun. The event is Saturday?"

"Ten to two," I confirmed.

"Great. I'll plan to attend. Right now, I should get going. The library opens in twenty minutes."

After Wilma left, Bree grabbed me by the arm. "Come with me. You have to see this."

I let Bree drag me down the hallway to her office. Tilly trailed along behind us. Sitting in the middle of Bree's desk was a beautiful bouquet of flowers. "Wow. That's some bouquet. Who's it from?"

Bree shrugged. "No idea. The delivery guy who brought it this morning said the flowers had been ordered and paid for by a source who wished to remain anonymous."

"Was there a card?"

"Just a small one that said, 'Happy Valentine's Day from a friend.' I love the mystery of an anonymous gift, but I'm dying to know who it's from. I've been racking my brain since it was delivered, but I can't think of a single person who would send such a wonderful bouquet."

Like Bree, I had no idea who would have sent the flowers, but I was grateful. Bree had been so depressed since her last boyfriend had been sent to prison after admitting to stealing an old man's life savings. It was good to see a smile on her face and a sparkle in her eye for the first time in weeks. "Maybe the flowers were sent by a customer? Or someone from book club?"

Bree tilted her head, causing her long blond hair to drape over her shoulder. "There are a couple of guys in book club who've asked me out, but I made it clear to each of them that I wasn't looking for a romantic entanglement at this point. I can't think of a single guy who would do something like this."

"I'm sure the flowers are just an icebreaker, and the man who sent them will follow up. In the meantime, enjoy the mystery."

Bree shrugged. "Yeah. I guess that makes sense. Are you coming to book club tonight?"

"If I can get the route done in time. I have a two-bagger today, so I'd best get going."

"Okay. Let me know if you aren't going to make it for some reason. Otherwise, I'll plan on you being there. If you want, we can get dinner after."

"I'd like that. I'll see you at six."

I left the bookstore and continued down the main street. I'd finished a quarter of the route and was nearing the halfway point, where I'd exchange my empty bag for the full one, when I got a text from Brady Baker, the new veterinarian in town. He asked if I had time to hand out some flyers for the Valentine party. I texted back that I had time to hand them out, but I didn't have time to pick them up. He texted that he would have Lilly meet me in midroute.

Lilly Long was Brady's new partner. She seemed to have been a good choice because she not only had been a practicing veterinarian for eight years, but she appeared to be a small-town girl at heart. She fit right in with the local crowd, which I knew was wonderful for Brady, but I wasn't sure how I felt about her living and working with White Eagle's most eligible bachelor. Brady and I were just friends, and he'd said on several occasions that he and Lilly were just friends as well, yet the thought of the two veterinarians spending so much time together caused a twinge of jealousy I couldn't rationally explain. I texted Brady again and informed him where I'd be, so Lilly could meet up with me. Then I slipped my phone into my pocket and continued on my route.

"Afternoon, Hap," I said to Hap Hollister as I entered his home and hardware store.

"Seems like you're late today," Hap said as I set his mail on the counter. When I only had one bag of mail to deliver, his store was one of my first deliveries.

"Double-bagger."

"I should have known. Lots of folks getting cards from their sweethearts, I imagine."

"Cards and packages. Have you decided what you're getting Hattie for Valentine's Day?"

Hattie Johnson was Hap's wife, or ex-wife, or something. To be honest, I wasn't sure exactly where they stood legally. What I did know was that Hap and Hattie used to be married, but they separated, or possibly divorced, a few years ago and moved into separate residences, but they continued to spend time together and went out on weekly dates.

"I'm struggling with that one a bit. We have our date night tonight. I'm hoping she'll drop a few hints as to what she'd like."

"Will you be taking her out on the big night?"

Hap frowned. "I'm not really clear on that. On one hand, our relationship agreement stipulates that Hattie will make dinner for me every Sunday, as well as on the seven major holidays, and in exchange, I'll take her on a proper date I plan and pay for every Wednesday and every other Saturday. The problem is, Valentine's Day is on Wednesday. Wednesday is my night to provide a date, but Valentine's Day is a holiday and therefore Hattie's day to cook for me."

"I guess you'll have to talk to her about it when you see her tonight."

"Yeah. I guess I will. By the way, I've been meaning to ask how Tang is doing. I miss the little guy now that he no longer does your route with you."

"He's doing well. I'll try to bring him by for a visit later in the week."

Tangletoe, or Tang for short, was an orange-and-white-striped kitten I found tangled up in some fishing wire just before Christmas. When I first found him, he was too young to be left alone, so Tilly carried Tang on the route with us in a backpack.

When he got a bit bigger, I knew it would no longer work to bring him everywhere I went the way I brought Tilly, so I adopted a buddy for him, a beautiful longhair black kitten named Tinder. Tang and Tinder seemed quite happy staying behind and destroying my cabin while Tilly and I delivered the mail.

Lilly was just pulling up into the loading zone in front of Cartwright's Furniture as I approached with the mail. I took a small detour to greet her at her car. The pretty woman with long black hair and huge brown eyes rolled down the driver's side window and handed me a stack of pink and white posters advertising the adoption event on Saturday.

"Brady say's thank you, as do I," Lilly said as I tucked the posters into my bag.

"Tilly and I are happy to help. It'll be wonderful to find homes for as many of the shelter residents as possible."

"I know you plan to show up early on Saturday." Lilly tucked a lock of her long hair behind one ear. "Do you think you'd have time to stop by the bakery on Saturday morning to pick up the cookies Brady ordered?"

"No problem at all. Did he order them from Hattie?"

Lilly nodded. "Five dozen heart-shaped sugar cookies with pink frosting. Hattie said she'd throw in a cooler of punch."

"Okay. I'll pick up the sweets and be at the high school by eight to help with the setup."

"Thanks, Tess. You're a peach."

Lilly rolled up her window and pulled into traffic while Tilly and I continued on our route. By the time

I'd delivered all the mail I'd been entrusted with for the day, it was almost five o'clock. I knew I'd have to hurry if I was going to make it home to change and drop off Tilly and make it back into town by six o'clock for book club. We'd had snow earlier in the week, so I couldn't drive too quickly; still, I pressed the speed limit just a bit so as not to be late. My cabin was located outside of town in a rural area off the highway. It's an old, dilapidated building on a large piece of land surrounded by forest that I wouldn't trade for anything. There are times during the winter when having such a long commute gets tiresome, but whenever I stand on my deck and listen to the sweet sound of nothing, I know I'm truly living in heaven.

I was just slowing down to navigate a tight curve when I heard a loud crash. I barely had time to apply my brakes when a deer ran onto the road ahead of me. I swerved to avoid hitting him, which caused me to fishtail before coming to a stop in the middle of the road. After taking a few deep breaths to calm my nerves, I slowly pulled onto the gravel shoulder, where a vehicle sat motionless. Based on the damage to the front end, the crash I'd heard must have been this vehicle hitting something just seconds before I arrived.

Books by Kathi Daley

Come for the murder, stay for the romance.

Zoe Donovan Cozy Mystery:
Halloween Hijinks
The Trouble With Turkeys
Christmas Crazy
Cupid's Curse
Big Bunny Bump-off
Beach Blanket Barbie
Maui Madness
Derby Divas
Haunted Hamlet
Turkeys, Tuxes, and Tabbies
Christmas Cozy
Alaskan Alliance
Matrimony Meltdown
Soul Surrender
Heavenly Honeymoon
Hopscotch Homicide
Ghostly Graveyard
Santa Sleuth
Shamrock Shenanigans
Kitten Kaboodle
Costume Catastrophe
Candy Cane Caper
Holiday Hangover
Easter Escapade
Camp Carter

Trick or Treason
Reindeer Roundup
Hippity Hoppity Homicide – March 2018

Zimmerman Academy The New Normal
Ashton Falls Cozy Cookbook

Tj Jensen Paradise Lake Mysteries by Henery Press:

Pumpkins in Paradise
Snowmen in Paradise
Bikinis in Paradise
Christmas in Paradise
Puppies in Paradise
Halloween in Paradise
Treasure in Paradise
Fireworks in Paradise
Beaches in Paradise – *June 2018*

Whales and Tails Cozy Mystery:

Romeow and Juliet
The Mad Catter
Grimm's Furry Tail
Much Ado About Felines
Legend of Tabby Hollow
Cat of Christmas Past
A Tale of Two Tabbies
The Great Catsby
Count Catula
The Cat of Christmas Present
A Winter's Tail
The Taming of the Tabby
Frankencat
The Cat of Christmas Future
Farewell to Felines– *February 2018*

Seacliff High Mystery:

The Secret
The Curse
The Relic
The Conspiracy
The Grudge
The Shadow
The Haunting

Sand and Sea Hawaiian Mystery:
Murder at Dolphin Bay
Murder at Sunrise Beach
Murder at the Witching Hour
Murder at Christmas
Murder at Turtle Cove
Murder at Water's Edge
Murder at Midnight

Writers' Retreat Southern Seashore Mystery:
First Case
Second Look
Third Strike
Fourth Victim
Fifth Night

Rescue Alaska Paranormal Mystery:
Finding Justice

A Tess and Tilly Mystery:
The Christmas Letter

Road to Christmas Romance:
Road to Christmas Past

USA Today best-selling author Kathi Daley lives in beautiful Lake Tahoe with her husband Ken. When she isn't writing, she likes spending time hiking the miles of desolate trails surrounding her home. She has authored more than seventy-five books in eight series, including Zoe Donovan Cozy Mysteries, Whales and Tails Island Mysteries, Sand and Sea Hawaiian Mysteries, Tj Jensen Paradise Lake Series, Writers' Retreat Southern Seashore Mysteries, Rescue Alaska Paranormal Mysteries, and Seacliff High Teen Mysteries. Find out more about her books at **www.kathidaley.com**

Stay up to date:

Newsletter, *The Daley Weekly* **http://eepurl.com/NRPDf**
Kathi Daley Blog – publishes each Friday
http://kathidaleyblog.com
Webpage – **www.kathidaley.com**
Facebook at Kathi Daley Books –
www.facebook.com/kathidaleybooks
Kathi Daley Books Group Page –
https://www.facebook.com/groups/569578823146850/
E-mail – **kathidaley@kathidaley.com**
Kathi_Daley
Twitter at Kathi Daley@kathidaley –
https://twitter.com/kathidaley
Amazon Author Page –
https://www.amazon.com/author/kathidaley
BookBub – **https://www.bookbub.com/authors/kathi-daley**

MAR 0 7 2018
South Lake Tahoe

Made in the USA
Columbia, SC
25 January 2018